SHADOW'S END

BROTHERHOOD PROTECTORS WORLD

SHADOW OPS SERIES

KATE MCKEEVER

This book is a work of fiction. Names, characters, places and incidents are products of the author's imagination or used fictitiously. Any resemblance to actual events, locales or persons living or dead is entirely coincidental.

Cover Art by Christine's Cover Creations

For my parents, as always. For the love of reading, the love of knowledge and the stubbornness to accomplish my goals.

Thank you to Karen Seaton for tush kicking, to Leanne Tyler for encouragement. I owe you desserts.

BROTHERHOOD PROTECTORS

ORIGINAL SERIES BY ELLE JAMES

Brotherhood Protectors Series

Montana SEAL (#1)

Bride Protector SEAL (#2)

Montana D-Force (#3)

Cowboy D-Force (#4)

Montana Ranger (#5)

Montana Dog Soldier (#6)

Montana SEAL Daddy (#7)

Montana Ranger's Wedding Vow (#8)

Montana SEAL Undercover Daddy (#9)

Cape Cod SEAL Rescue (#10)

Montana SEAL Friendly Fire (#11)

Montana SEAL's Mail-Order Bride (#12)

SEAL Justice (#13)

Ranger Creed (#14)

Delta Force Rescue (#15)

Dog Days of Christmas (#16)

Montana Rescue (#17)

Montana Ranger Returns (#18)

Hot SEAL Salty Dog (SEALs in Paradise)

Hot SEAL Hawaiian Nights (SEALs in Paradise)

Hot SEAL Bachelor Party (SEALs in Paradise)

CHAPTER 1

Elise Fanning lifted the night scope and stared through it, searching for her target. Felix Varela strode from the private airplane hangar with confidence she found infuriating, considering he was on her own soil. The South American drug dealer had eluded her and her team for months now, usually leaving a town just as they arrived. Intelligence indicated no mole, but superior planning on his part. He'd arranged for multiple routes for travel while he was in the states and they'd played cat and mouse, guessing each time he left a location, trying to find him, wasting valuable time and manpower on surveillance and coverage. At least he hadn't left the country when he'd found them hunting for him.

Why he'd stayed in the U.S. was a mystery, but one she was grateful for. Even if the DEA had oversea stations, foreign laws were an obstacle she didn't want to deal with.

Elise studied her team. Anderson was covering the east side of the parking area in front of the hangar, deep in the shadows. Garcia and his men had the west side covered. Her own men had insured the rear of the building was free of personnel, friendly and not so much. Now, she only had to make her move, secure the first of three arrests and her career, her purpose for joining the DEA, would be made.

She motioned for the team to move out and silently crept from her spot, her weapon steady in her hand. Then all hell broke loose.

The shots came from three directions, just out of the zone of coverage and Elise cursed under her breath as she saw Anderson go down clutching his leg. Another member sidestepped around him, heading for cover from the barrage of weapon fire. Elise kept her eye on the target, watching as a shadow moved back toward the hangar. Varela's bulk moved with his characteristic limp as he made his way back to safety. Elise picked up her pace, running now, darting from parked car to car, hoping she'd make it in time.

The SUV almost hit her on the way out. The lights blinded her for a second and she dove to the side, feeling the rush of air from the vehicle passing her. Pebbles dug into her bare arms and she cursed, aloud this time. It didn't matter who heard her now. The kingpin was in the fleeing vehicle.

"Garcia! He's in the black SUV." She hissed through her mic, only to be met with silence.

"Garcia. Jimmy?"

"He's down, ma'am." The voice over the earpiece sent a shard of cold through her.

"Bad?"

"Yeah." That tone told her everything. If her best man was not dead yet, he was close. Elise rolled to a sitting position and then stood, barking out a command for status as she did so. Two down, the rest of the team okay. As she hurried toward her injured comrades, she sent up a swift prayer that she wasn't going to be responsible for her friend's death.

Hours later, Elise sat in a hospital waiting room in Houston, anxious for word of her team members. She still bore the stains of trying to staunch the persistent flow of blood from Garcia's chest wound while they waited for the ambulance. She eyed the clock. It had been three hours since he'd been taken into surgery and she'd fielded calls and texts from her superiors since. Anderson, while not in a life-threatening condition, had been admitted and faced surgery as well, his wound in the knee. After a quick look and queasiness, Elise worried that he'd face a long recuperation. And would he be able to return to the field, as he'd wish to do?

She glanced at her phone again and responded to her supervisor's text. She didn't have any news to share, other than Garcia was still alive. She'd put off calling his wife, knowing he'd not want Caitlyn to know until there was definitive news. Still, Elise wondered, wouldn't she want to know? She stared at her phone then pulled up her contacts, her finger hovering over Caitlyn's number.

"Ms. Fanning?" The doctor wore sweat-stained scrubs and his eyes were weary. Sporting a predawn scruff, he looked as exhausted as Elise felt. She stood and gave him her full attention, stuffing her phone into her black khaki pants pocket. "Yes."

"Your colleague is out of surgery." He sat in the chair, flopping as if he had no strength left. "We almost lost him a couple of times but he's strong."

"Will he make it?" she asked.

"We'll see. The next couple of days will tell the tale. He had a collapsed lung and the bullet also grazed his heart, which complicates matters. If we can control the internal bleeding from that we'll be lucky."

"I need to inform his wife of his condition, doctor, and she'll want to come here."

He looked down at his hands for a long moment then turned dark eyes toward her, his voice grave.

"Call her now. She needs to get here as soon as she can."

Elise dialed Caitlyn and spent several minutes both trying to calm her friend's wife and encourage her to get on a plane asap. After another call to the main office to expedite Caitlyn's travel, she made a third call. This time it was to the one man she knew could help her find Varela.

KANE REYNOLDS LEANED back in his chair and out of the window across from his desk, watching the rain fall in sheets. Monsoon season in Georgia. He reasoned that his mood was affected by the rain but then, again, whose wasn't?

It had been raining in the desert the night Penny died. The thought caught him unawares and he waited for the pang of grief to overcome him, surprised when all he felt was regret, but not surprised by the guilt. If he'd only had a better feel of the situation, he reminded himself again, his wife wouldn't have been shot, wouldn't have bled to death in the middle of nowhere. Wouldn't have left him with the deed undone.

He shifted in his chair, trying to slough off the dread that accompanied memories of Penny and their short marriage. Instead, he found Hank Patterson's number and called his old friend, sure he'd be able to redirect his thoughts.

"Hey, Kane. What's up?"

"Just calling to check in and see how the foreign base investigation is going," Kane picked up a pen and started clicking it, the sound loud in his office.

"We've found several of the connections overseas. The problem is, when we let the military officials know, they move in and arrest one guy and the organization has someone to replace him before a week is out." Hank's frustration came through the line.

"Which we anticipated." Kane agreed. "Have you been able to trace the source?"

"No." Hank's curt response told Kane more than a detailed answer would. Hank's team of bodyguards/security specialists had been on the case of drug distribution to foreign military bases months before he'd become involved. Hank had pulled him in to do the ghost work on the case and he'd been totally invested ever since.

"Want me to pull in some guys on my end?" Kane said and clicked his pen again, grimacing when the pen fell apart in his hand. He tossed the pieces onto the desk and opened the center drawer, extracting another pen.

"Nah. I've got my tech guys on it. I think we can find a link electronically. Then we'll put in the legwork."

Kane had forgone the clicking of a pen to pulling open the cap of this pen with his thumb then pushing the thing closed again, repeatedly. He huffed a sigh. "Sometimes I wish we were back in the sandbox. It was a lot more cut and dry then."

"Except when it wasn't," Hank drawled and Kane had to laugh. They'd been knee-deep in the stinky stuff more than once during their tours together. "Right. Well, let me know if I can do anything with the situation."

They disconnected soon afterward and Kane opened a file he'd been working on earlier in the day. Rivera and Franklin, two of his best agents in the middle east, had been compromised and to be extracted. Now, he had to figure out what to do with them. Both agents were excellent at their jobs, antsy to get back in the field, and a liability while they were in the states. He'd learned from hard experience that the type of person who worked for him and did an exceptional job was also the type of person that didn't stay idle long. And if he didn't fill that need for excitement, purpose, and adrenaline then they would, either for good or bad.

When the phone rang, he stared at it, wondering at the zing in his nerves at the sound. Not surprise, nor apprehension. Anticipation? He lifted the secure phone and answered.

"Reynolds."

"Kane? It's Elise Fanning. I need your help."

CHAPTER 2

Kane stood at the edge of the private airstrip, his eyes covered with sunglasses, both to dampen the intensity of the Georgia sun and to keep the flying grit from his eyes. He watched as the small plane landed smoothly on the tarmac and then taxied to the end of the runway. As he strode to the aircraft, a door opened and the connected stairs dropped down. A single figure stepped from the plane and strode down the steps.

Elise Fanning, lean and dressed in a white blouse, dark pants, and jacket, looked the epitome of a federal agent and was. Kane's research from months before had impressed him. The woman had one aim, to be the best DEA agent she could be, and had succeeded in the fifteen years or so she'd been in the organization. Certainly, she'd been in the field longer than many of her cohorts.

As she walked toward him, a tendril escaped her low ponytail and caught on her mouth and Kane was surprised at the spurt of attraction he felt as he watched her brush it away. He admired the woman for her skills but had never noticed her efficient grace and attractiveness before. Her blue eyes, intent and steady, now hidden behind dark lenses, could pin a witness with their chill but he had to wonder if they could burn with something else?

He held out his hand to shake hers. "Welcome to Shadow Ops."

She shook his hand and then pulled hers away in a quick move. "Thanks, and thanks for agreeing to meet in person. I've gotten pretty paranoid over the last couple of months about communication."

"Do you have any luggage?" he asked, noting she only carried a business satchel over her shoulder. She shook her head. "I'm planning on flying back tonight."

He mentally shrugged and led the way to his SUV, opening the passenger door for her before rounding the vehicle and getting inside. As he headed to the small state road and the circuitous route to his headquarters he mentally reviewed their agenda.

Rather than discussing the case in the car, Kane asked about her agents. "Garcia is still in critical condition," she said, her tone flat. "He's in Brownsville with his wife and will probably stay there for a bit. Anderson was transferred back to Seattle where he's going to have surgery on his knee."

"Total?" Kane asked, meaning would Anderson need a total replacement of the joint. Elise shrugged. "Maybe. The slug could have done enough damage. The doctors don't think it did enough vascular damage to warrant amputation, but it wasn't pretty."

Now Kane understood her request for his help. Two of her best agents and probably friends had been wounded to the point that their careers had been interrupted, if not their lives. As someone who supervised others, he knew too well how much responsibility he'd felt when someone was injured. And when someone died—

They arrived at the sprawling land he'd bought when he'd left government work. Mountains in the near distance seemed wreathed in the haze from the atmosphere and Kane was soon turning onto the one lane road leading to his home and base.

He'd found twenty acres in the foothills of the north Georgia mountains and had found the one place he felt peace for any period of time. As the road wound through the gentle slopes of the pasture and then up a small swell, he eyed the surroundings. Fencing, innocuous and wired with security alerts, circled his land and interspersed were small copses of trees, again with concealed cameras, mics, and proximity alerts. While he could be considered by many as paranoid, in his line of business, both past and present, he needed every bit of the covert security he could buy. The main building, a squat concrete building that put one in mind of a warehouse, sat back behind more trees and had fencing around it to hide the vehicles, equipment, and other structures. His own house, a brick rancher with working storm shutters sprawled beyond.

Instead of taking Elise to the security building, he headed to the house and the small lunch his housekeeper/assistant had prepared. He pulled into the garage, leaving the door open behind him.

Elise eyed the land around them as she exited the SUV. "This is different."

Kane grinned knowingly, "What did you expect? A big military outpost? A sign? Men and women running obstacle courses?"

She blushed and grinned back at him. "Something like that."

"We specialize in covert, remember? My building has tractors and farm implements, all used and seen regularly on the land, planting and harvesting. It's all just a north Georgia retired military man, getting back in touch with the land."

She laughed. "You drive a tractor?"

He opened a rear door to the house and motioned her inside before clicking a button beside the door. As he went into the house behind her a steel reinforced garage door lowered.

"I drive it occasionally, enough for the odd passerby or neighbor to see me actually on the land. I also have a couple of people who work the land for me. The retired part, you know."

She shook her head. "You have people believing you are a retired guy that lazes around? You look too young, too buff."

Again, he grinned as she blushed. He knew he looked his age but a regimen of workouts kept him fit. In his soul, he was ancient and sometimes felt it. Except when he could laugh with others, like now.

"I'm also a retiree that travels, remember? I'm off fishing and sailing, visiting old friends and so on." The tales of the big catch always guaranteed a good cover for his overseas missions.

She followed him into the farm kitchen where his assistant, Faith, was hard at work at the counter. "Sounds like you've got it figured out."

"That part, maybe," he replied.

Faith turned at their entrance and smiled. She was shorter than Elise and rounded in a way that belied any thought of trained military personnel. Her jeans fit perfectly and she wore a knit shirt that was tucked in, revealing a waist that Elise envied. "Great, you're right on time. "

She turned and revealed a platter of food that made Elise's stomach rumble. Cuts of ham, turkey, and other assorted meats ranged the outer areas of the platter, with vegetables on the inner. Other plates with pieces of bread, condiments, and chips filled the counter, as well as bottled water and what looked like a pitcher of iced tea. Faith fanned a hand across the food. "Dig in, the plates are there. I'll see you later."

She left them standing at the counter. Kane stepped forward and started filling a plate then looked at Elise. "Not hungry?"

She mentally shook off the shock of jealousy she'd felt at realizing Kane had a partner and stepped forward to fill her plate. "Thanks for this. I didn't realize I was hungry."

"And you probably haven't eaten since before the sting."

She frowned, aware he was right.

He motioned to the farm table in the center of the room and she laid her plate down before turning. "I'd like to wash my hands first."

"Sorry. Down the hall to the left."

As she went to the bathroom, Elise glanced around the house. The great room was open and masculine looking with wooden paneling and tan leather seating. The hall didn't sport anything more than a bookcase at its end and a large framed photo of verdant green mountains. The bathroom, serviceable and up to date with fixtures, had gray and tan towels, a neutral scented handwash, and more nature prints. If the woman was his wife or partner, she certainly didn't contribute to the decorating scheme.

Back in the kitchen, Kane had poured a couple of glasses of iced tea and also put a bottled water near her plate. She sat and took a drink of the tea then grimaced. "Wow, that's sweet."

He laughed and took a sip of his own. "It takes some getting used to. When I first moved here, I refused to have it in the house but Faith infiltrated it into the meals. Now, I'll drink a glass a day to satisfy the Georgia requirement."

Elise had uncapped the water and taken a cleansing draft. "I've drunk tea before. It's not as sweet as this."

"Nothing is," he chuckled then set in on his lunch.

They ate silently for a few minutes. After the initial hunger was alleviated, Kane wiped his mouth with a napkin and looked at Elise. "Tell me about your operation."

She sighed and laid down the sandwich then wiped her hands. "I don't think we have a mole. After the last few months and the whole debacle Agent Simpson went through, I've been diligent with background checks, checking bank balances, everything. I pulled in agents I trust with my life, agents I've worked with for years. And the plans for arrest, any movement isn't filtered through the normal channels. So, if there is a mole, he or she is better than me." She eyed Kane. "Varela is my case and I've had total control over who has access to information. Two other agents were assigned the other two leaders. Every time I think I'm going to get him, he slips out of my hands. This last time in Brownsville, I was closest I've ever been."

"Do you know where he went?"

She shook her head. "He flew out under the radar, of course, so no tracking that way. I haven't had any news that he's out of the country but when he took off he was heading south, so he may be in Mexico or South America."

"I doubt that," Kane said, surprising Elise. She shot him a questioning look and he indicated the food. "Finish up. I have some things to share with you about Mr. Varela."

She tossed her napkin onto her half-filled plate and pushed her chair back. "Tell me."

He smiled slightly and then stood. "Let's go into my office and we'll talk."

After they'd found seats in the oh-so-masculine office, Elise eyed the spacious yet austere surroundings. "Your wife sure doesn't have a lot of input on your furnishings or does she like early caveman as well?"

From his reaction she knew she'd stuck her foot in her mouth. "My wife never saw this house. She was killed a couple of years before I bought the land."

"Oh, sorry." Elise felt yet another flush move over her face. "I thought—"

"Faith is my assistant. She also does light house-cleaning and prepares light lunches like we had today." He leaned back in his chair and eyed Elise closely. "You thought she was my wife? She's at least fifteen years my junior."

Elise shrugged. "Doesn't seem to matter."

"It does to me. I don't want to be involved with someone who doesn't have the same memories of youth that I have." He straightened and Elise could almost see him shake himself out of a mood and turn his attention to the topic she should have stayed on, Varela.

"Tell me what you know about Varela," she prompted and he nodded then stood and retrieved a sheaf of papers.

"I dug around after Hank and I talked earlier today." At her apparent surprise, he continued. "I've been trying to keep updated on the investigation, just in case. Anyway, I got the names from Hank of the leaders of the drug distribution ring to the foreign bases. Hank has been able to impact some of the bases but he hasn't had much luck with the leaders, since he has limited personnel he can devote to the foreign end of things. I, on the other

hand, have ninety percent of my personnel in foreign countries."

He handed Elise a sheet with bulleted points and as she reviewed them he expounded. "You probably know most of this by now, but here's what I found out. Varela started out as a mule for one of the drug cartels in South America. He moved up in rank through attrition by murder. Some was his doing, some other by disgruntled middlemen. He's ruthless, power-hungry, and absolutely without any allegiance except to himself. Even his family members aren't exempt."

Elise nodded as she read an example of Varela's ambition. He'd had his brother-in-law murdered for holding back monies due to him. His family members no longer worked for him, either because he didn't trust them or they no longer wanted to take the chance. She was surprised when she saw that most of his family had fled to central America and lived in near-poverty conditions while Varela was a millionaire many times over.

"That's interesting but doesn't tell me why he'd not return to Mexico or South America."

"He has at least three contracts out on him in South America, one in Mexico. Anyone who wants to advance in the drug trade, earn respect amongst the workers, will be on his tail as soon as he enters the country."

"But he's way more powerful than any of them,"

she said and closed the file. "He can hire the best security there is."

Kane shrugged, "Or he can fly out to any of the Caribbean islands, a couple of other countries that turn blind eyes to drugs, and relax and regroup without having to worry about his back any more than usual." At her look of doubt, he tilted his head, "I just have a gut feeling he doesn't want to deal with his old stomping grounds. In his eyes, he's moved beyond them."

She turned the page and reviewed a list of properties Varela was rumored to own. Europe, Australia, and even a small island in the South Pacific. "No properties in Central or South America?"

Kane shook his head, "The family was poor when he was growing up, didn't own any property then and anything he had on the way up was sold off about a dozen years ago when he moved into military distribution."

Twelve years? Elise hadn't had a record of the length of time Varela had been involved in distributing drugs to the military. Twelve years meant a lot of lives were impacted. She laid the papers in her lap and sighed. "You know what all this means, don't you?"

He nodded, "A lot of work for us."

Elise acknowledged her relief as her stomach unclenched. "You'll help, then?"

He stood and held out his hand for the papers then took them to his desk and placed them in a file and closed it. "I've been on the periphery of this investigation for months, Elise. I want in and I want to catch these men. I want to make them pay."

CHAPTER 3

If Elise was surprised at his use of her first name, she didn't show it. They'd only called each other by their last names in the past, but now, something had changed. Either her awareness of him or his of her, or both. He didn't question the why or how, he only knew she was more important to him now than she had been before and it scared him more than the thought of going after Varela did.

They talked for several hours, unaware of the passing of time until a knock on the door interrupted them. Faith waited for Kane's response and opened the door only far enough to stand at the edge of the room. "I'm off for the day, Kane, unless you need anything else."

He glanced at his watch then shook his head. "Thanks for letting me know. See you tomorrow." She nodded and closed the door after her.

"I'd better get in touch with the pilot," Elise muttered, her eyes on the view outside his window. The summer light still showed through the panes and if she approached the window, Kane knew she'd feel the warmth that radiated from the summer heat outside. He stretched in the chair, suddenly aware of the stiffness that had set in from sitting so long. "We still have a lot to discuss."

"I know but I didn't plan on staying more than the day."

"Do you have meetings tomorrow? Have to be back in Seattle?"

She shook her head, "I'm in Brownsville for the time being." She paused for a second then he saw the resolution in her eyes. "I'll let the pilot know I'm staying overnight."

He watched as she wrote a text and responded to a couple more. He ignored the satisfaction of knowing she'd be there, in his house, for the night. When she started punching in another text, he asked, "Someone in the office?"

"No. I need to find a place to stay overnight and a rental." She didn't look up as she continued her search. When he put his hand over hers to stop her keying in, she glanced up in question. "I have plenty of space and extra toothbrushes. If you need anything else I can have Faith pick it up and bring it out to the house."

"That's not necessary," she began only to stop

when he held up his hand. "Please, stay. As I said, I have plenty of room and other agents stay here often, it's not that big of a deal. And why I always have extra deodorant and the odd item of clothing around. And Faith is used to making some trips out in the evenings, I pay her handsomely for the task."

Elise's expression puzzled him but he turned and headed back to the desk. "Let me get Faith on the line and you can tell her what you need. We'll order up a meal too, while we're at it."

A couple hours later, Elise found herself in a roomy but somewhat sterile bedroom. The white comforter reminded her of a nice hotel's bed covering. In fact, the whole room gave her a hotel vibe, with the upholstered easy chair and side table in one corner, a lamp for reading and a desk for computer work if she wished. All in all, comfortable but without any personality. She laid the tote bag of toiletries and underwear she'd requested on the bed, along with the extra blouse she hadn't. When Faith showed up, she'd had the blouse on a hanger, pressed and ready to don the next morning. She'd also bought a couple of options in sleepwear, a sleepshirt and a pair of pajamas. Elise gratefully accepted the package and wondered idly why she hadn't thought to bring her go bag on the trip. Had she subconsciously wanted to stay as distant as she could from Kane Reynolds? She'd acknowledged her attraction to him from the beginning of their association when he'd helped with security and apprehension of several middlemen in the drug distribution ring. But she'd also realized that, as a private security provider and one that skirted the edge of legality at that, he wasn't someone she needed to pursue a relationship with.

She took the toiletries to the en suite bathroom and unpacked them, then hung the blouse in the empty closet. As she eyed the pajamas, she smiled to herself. A knit knee-length sleepshirt with a lamb on its front and cotton thigh-length shorts with a prim button-up short sleeve blouse. No way was either of the options clothing that was designed to ignite a man's imagination or desire. Kane may think he was too old for Faith, but she'd bet her sidearm that Faith didn't agree.

She headed back downstairs to the great room, where she and Kane had retreated after his call to Faith. He'd made them coffee and they'd talked about Varela and their options for an hour more before Faith arrived. Now, the great room was empty and she went in search of Kane.

He stood at the counter, taking a lid from a foil container, releasing a tantalizing scent of Italian spice and tomato sauce. Three other containers sat on the counter, along with plates. "I ordered lasagna and salad," he said and produced a spatula with which he started squaring up the lasagna. Elise came to stand beside him and breathed in the scent of oregano, basil, and deliciousness. "It smells great."

"From a little hole in the wall, in the middle of nowhere. Best food around." He said and motioned to the other containers. "Salad and dessert."

She unwrapped the container of salad to reveal Caesar salad. A tiny cardboard bowl nestled in the corner which, uncapped, revealed croutons. The third container held several pastries that looked and smelled heavenly.

They served themselves at the bar, already seeming to fall into an easy routine, then headed to the table which held wine glasses and the ubiquitous pitcher of tea. Elise laughed and shook her head at his offer to pour her a glass and indicated the wine instead. "I think I can handle one glass of that then I'll have to switch to water or coffee for the evening round of planning."

Kane's hand hesitated only a moment before he poured their wine. They talked of the restaurant and its owner, a transplant from Chicago who'd traveled south looking for warmer winters. "We get some cold weather here but it's nothing to the stuff he was used to."

"Was he a chef in Chicago?" Elise asked, a filled fork on its way to her mouth.

"Nope. A firefighter. Used his retirement funds to move down here and realized there weren't any restaurants in the area, other than the ones near the interstate. Opened his place a few years ago and apparently does well enough to stay open.

"If this food is any indication, he should be okay." She sighed and looked at her now empty plate, wondering if she could justify a second helping. Kane offered her one but she declined. "I want to save some room for a pastry later."

He got another, smaller, piece of lasagna and returned to his seat. She noticed he'd grabbed a couple of waters from the fridge on his way back and accepted one from him.

"Do you cook at all?" She asked, uncapping her bottle and relaxing back into her chair.

He shook his head. "I can do scrambled eggs and toast, sometimes don't burn the bacon. I have frozen dinners I buy from Frank, the guy that sent us the lasagna. And I do sandwiches a lot. Never found the time or inclination to cook." He glanced up from his plate. "You?"

"Enough to get by. I don't experiment with cooking. I've never had the time. I can make basic foods, chicken and rice, breakfast foods, and a decent steak or fish dish. Life in the agency doesn't mix with domesticity."

He nodded. "Not enough time in the day to work out, research, get the files done."

"Not to mention the travel and training," Elise

added, realizing they both spoke with the same tired tone. "Not that I regret the job."

"No, but sometimes, it gets old. Or it did for me. It's one of the reasons I went out on my own." He pushed his plate away and took a sip of his water.

"And has it been as satisfying as you expected?" she asked, her curiosity genuine.

"Yes and no. I like being independent but some of the cases... Well, let's just say I'm not sure I'm doing that much good."

Elise fiddled with the label on the water bottle, her thoughts on the arrests, near misses, and failed attempts to stop the flow of drugs into the country. Had her efforts, along with her cohorts, been effective? She sighed and glanced up to see Kane watching her with jaded, knowing eyes. "You ever want to quit?" he asked quietly.

"Every day." She said and stood, taking her plate to the sink to rinse. As she did, she became aware of him following her, opening the dishwasher, and placing his utensils in the basket. They finished the cleanup together and wandered back to the great room, both lost in their thoughts.

"What would I do, if I quit?" Elise continued the conversation when she was seated on the leather sofa. Kane joined her there rather than taking his earlier seat in an easy chair. "I have a certain skill set that isn't necessarily made for civilian life. I can shoot well, track people, organize tactical teams."

She laughed dryly. "If I left the agency, I'd be looking for jobs in security or an agency like yours. Not much different than what I do now."

He nodded and stretched, his gaze going to the ceiling as he straightened his long legs and crossed his ankles. "I've wondered myself. I guess I could become that farmer we talked about. The land could make enough to get by, along with my savings and retirement from the Navy. But that'd probably drive me crazy."

She tilted her head in agreement. "Once you're an adrenaline junkie, it doesn't go away, does it?"

"Only by necessity." He shook his head and levered upright, turning to grin at her. "Let's get back to work. All this navel-gazing and what-iffing is making me depressed."

She nodded, "Can we have some coffee? That meal almost did me in."

They made their way to the kitchen for coffee and then to his office. There, Kane found a message light blinking on his phone. He returned the call and then grinned at Elise. "Thanks, Greg. I'll get back with you soon."

Elise raised a brow at his grin. "What?"

"We have a location. Wanta go for a ride?"

CHAPTER 4

ELISE STARED at the small jet and then at Kane. "We're flying?"

He nodded and waved at the man who'd taxied the plane from its hangar at the small airport she'd arrived at that morning. When he began to inspect the exterior of the plane she hurried after him. "Where are we going?"

"Laredo." He ran his hands along the flaps of the wings and then bent to inspect the body's fuselage. Elise rounded the wing to stand in front of him. "Hold it." When he didn't respond, she grabbed his forearm and brought him to a halt. "Kane! Talk to me. I'm not going anywhere until I have an update."

He straightened, his frown letting her know he didn't like being confronted. Then his face cleared and he ran a hand down his face before relaxing.

"Sorry, I'm used to giving orders, I guess. Let's take a walk and I'll fill you in."

She strode alongside him down the tarmac, aware of his divided attention between her and the state of the runway. "I called a contact earlier today and had him put out some feelers on Varela."

"When? I've been with you all day and you didn't make any calls," she asked, her natural wariness showing itself.

"When you were upstairs, in your bedroom. Anyway, Greg is an old friend of Hank's and mine from the SEALs and has a small security firm in Texas. He does a lot of surveillance work and has some contacts along the border. He found out that Varela was seen on the Mexican side of the border near Laredo. I figured you wouldn't want anyone else to do the work."

Elise nodded, her head down, her eyes unseeing as they walked. The border town of Laredo had as big of a drug interdiction problem as all of the other southern Texas towns. It made sense that Varela might want to stay close to his supply sources but then, what about the animosity Kane had brought up earlier? She mentioned that and he shook his head. "Not sure. Maybe he's thinking he can take care of the situation or doesn't seem to think anyone can touch him."

"It's the latter," she said, her knowledge of the

drug kingpin enough to know of his massive ego. "Okay, let's get on the road, or in the air, as it were. Who's flying?"

He grinned and with a hand on her back, turned back in the direction of the plane. "I've flown since before I left the military. Got my license for my thirtieth birthday."

"I'll need more stuff," she said under her breath as they boarded the plane. Men. They never planned ahead.

Kane urged her to sit with him in the cockpit and she agreed, not wanting to have the spacious six-seat passenger area to herself. As she settled into the plane she reminded Kane he could have given her some notice to bring along her things. He gestured toward the rear storage area behind the seats. "Got clothes, toiletries, extra provisions stored in the rear."

"And weapons? Ammo?" she asked.

"Will be waiting for us when we get to Laredo." He continued the flight check and Elise let him do his work. She opened her satchel and removed her phone. She made some notes and sent a single text to the single member of her own team left uninjured, letting him know she'd be out of pocket for a couple of days. As she hit send she felt Kane's eyes on her. "I let my team know I'll be on the road for a bit."

"Trustworthy?" He said and turned his attention back to taxiing to the end of the asphalt runway.

"Very." She quelled the resentment the one-word question elicited but understood it. The whole investigation had been riddled with moles and people paid off by the drug cartel. To think that another member of the DEA or other federal agency could be on Varela's payroll, as well as the two other leaders, wasn't out of the realm of possibility.

They were silent as Kane focused on taking off, confirming his route with the small tower, and getting to a cruising altitude. Elise didn't mind flying, had done a lot of it during her career and before, as a rather privileged college student. Still, she wondered at the sense of ease she felt in the small plane. Kane handled the compact jet as if he were sitting in his easy chair at his home, secure in his knowledge of its function.

"How long before we get to Laredo?"

"A little over a couple of hours. Greg's going to meet us at the airstrip and we'll head out from there."

She nodded, her mind racing through the needed supplies. "I can call in some of my team members and have them meet us there. What are the coordinates?"

He told her the coordinates for the small private

and she conveyed that to White, the only other member she'd trust. He texted his plan to head out with men immediately. She'd arrive before they would, he told her, but he'd be there. When she turned her attention back to Kane, he had the automatic pilot engaged and had pulled a backpack from under his seat and had it resting on his lap. He extracted a small device from the pack and opened it.

Elise leaned forward to get a closer look and he motioned to the compact drone. "We can use it as an extra team member."

Elise glanced at the setting sun and then back at the drone. "Won't do any good tonight."

"It has infrared. I've used it and so have my men. It's good." He finished checking the drone and then extracted another small device, which turned out to be a tracker. How he'd get a pin on someone to track them, Elise didn't know and hadn't the brain power to figure out right now, but she watched him go through several other gadgets, explaining them as he did. "Compact computer system, virtually bug proof. Night glasses, not as bulky as goggles. Simple supplies including tear gas and zip ties, cloths to use as gags. The latter surprised Elise until Kane explained. "Remember, most of my agents go in silently and come out the same way. If we need the target conscious, we also need them silent." The last item he pulled from the backpack was a syringe that appeared to be an Epipen. All of these he started slipping into two different tactical belts, dividing them evenly and, Elise knew, strategically. Finally, he placed the loaded belts in the backpack and tucked them back under his seat. Elise smiled wryly. "I feel vastly unprepared."

"Just taken by surprise," he said and unbuckled his seatbelt. When he stood, she quickly took a look at the horizon indicator. She might not know a lot about planes, but she knew to look there. The plane was nice and steady as Kane stepped away from the pilot seat and to the storage unit. As Elise watched, not ready to admit a building anxiety at the sight of the only one who could land this sucker out of the command chair, he extracted two bulletproof vests and then headed back to the front of the plane. Once there, he handed her a vest and shrugged on the other. She donned the vest as he reseated himself and then checked the controls. "We'll be there within the hour, so let's review our plans."

"Okay. My men are about an hour behind us, but if Varela is still in Mexico, we'll have time to plan and execute."

"If. We knew his whereabouts a little over an hour ago but who knows where he's gone since. What about the other two leaders of the ring? Are they in communication with Varela?"

"I don't think so. Maybe. We haven't had any luck getting info on communications, other than within his outer circle. We've been one step behind him the entire time I've been chasing him. Brownsville was the closest I'd gotten to him."

"Let's put in a call to Hank, see what he has to say." Kane retrieved his phone and placed it in a holder on the upper part of the control panel. He made the call and Hank's face appeared within seconds. "Hey, what's up?"

"Elise Fanning and I are on our way to Laredo, got a tip on Varela."

"Agent," Hank said, his mouth quirking in a half smile. Elise acknowledged him and then asked. "Have your team members had any luck in finding communication links between Varela, Novak, and Brown?"

"No. We've concentrated more on the foreign bases. That's a whopping big hole in our plan." His self-disgust was evident without noting the look on his face and Elise nodded. "We've been looking at it on our end but to be honest with you, my efforts have been focused mainly on Varela. He's the one who's been the most active. The US and European leaders haven't blipped at all on our radar."

"Nor mine," Kane added, surprising Elise. She knew he'd shared an interest in the investigation, but he hadn't admitted to active involvement before. Hank's next comment brought her out of her reverie, and she turned her attention back to him. "I'll put in a call to Senator Mitchell." Hank said. "He's been calling in favors right and left to get some intel for us."

"He should have some," Kane murmured, his hands returning to the controls of the plane. Elise felt a slight dip in the plane as he turned the automatic pilot off and took control of the flight again. "Let us know as soon as you find out anything?"

"Will do. You need anything for Laredo?"

"No. Elise and I have it covered from our end," Kane said, and they soon ended the call. She shut her satchel and tucked it under her seat. As the dark horizon revealed a tiny speck of light, she realized they were getting close to the landing site. She mentally switched gears and became the efficient DEA agent with over a decade of experience.

A man dressed in black pants and a short sleeve black t-shirt stood with his arms crossed over his chest as they taxied to the small hangar lit from inside. The open doors revealed several people milling around, carrying backpacks, stooping to pick up small chests, and generally getting ready for an attack or advance. Elise realized the man sitting beside her was vastly more experienced than she at logistics. While she could call a team together, plan an operation and execute it, she didn't have dozens of men at her disposal just from a call. Her job, bureaucracy at its best, required paperwork to acquire any of the equipment he'd produced from under his seat and would have taken several days to be delivered. Kane Reynolds, she knew, ran an organization equal to a small army and had arms that could access other similar organizations. She'd been glad she'd called him before, but now she was doubly grateful. Maybe something would get done and she'd deal with the fallout from her bosses later.

Kane greeted Greg with a handshake and nodded toward the men and women in the hangar. "Everything go okay?"

Greg followed his gaze. "Yeah. Franklin and Rivera got here about half an hour ago. Drove in from outside of San Antonio."

Kane nodded. He'd sent the two to Texas on a whim, knowing a little of Varela's movements. Now, with them on an active team, he could be assured of coverage, as well as giving them a way to let off the steam that built up between assignments. He greeted the small darkly tanned Rivera who grinned at him as he strapped on a shoulder holster. "Got something for us to do, boss? I was about to go off."

"I'll keep you busy, Teo. Where'd Tom get to?"

"He's checking out the lights." Teo gestured to the rear of the hangar and a closed door. After reassuring the wiry ex-soldier he'd be in the thick of the action, Kane headed for the back of the structure. Opening the door, he watched as the other orphan member of his team, a burly redhead with a now bushy beard flick small penlights on and off in succession. After a couple more minutes, Tom Franklin turned and gave Kane a solemn nod. "All good, sir."

"You good too, Tom?"

"A little antsy this past week or so, but good to go, now, sir." Tom had been out of the military for three years but never got past the urge to salute and sir every man he considered his superior. The fact that he hadn't saluted a couple of colonels during his service had branded him a shirker. He was one of Kane's best men and a very dangerous man on and off the field.

"We're going to have a briefing in about ten," Kane said and left Franklin to finish his review of the equipment.

When he joined Elise and Greg, he noted her putting her phone back in her pocket. "Your men?"

"About fifteen minutes away." She swiped a strand of hair out of her eyes and glanced at the tactical equipment. "Want to go over some of the equipment with me?"

He did and then retrieved the tactical belts he'd prepared from the plane. When he handed one to her, she glanced up in surprise. "Do I need all of this?"

"Can you operate all of that?" he countered, and

she pulled each item from the belt, demonstrated the use and activation of same, and then put them back and gave him the side eye. He grinned. "You might never need them but they're handy if you do. And we'll get wired for communication after your guys arrive."

She glanced at the equipment again and sighed. "Boy, to be a privateer like you."

"It has its advantages," he drawled. Chief of which was that he didn't have to answer to anyone, other than the government for the big things like kills and such. And sometimes, what the government didn't know didn't matter.

Her team arrived fifteen minutes later and piled out of the SUV looking armed and ready. Two men and a woman, all with blazers covering bulletproof vests underneath their shirts. Kane noticed one of the men looking nervous and decided to team him with Rivera. He'd be able to look after the guy and make sure he was on the up and up.

The team, consisting of Elise's three agents, Kane's two, and the two of them, met up in the middle of the room. Greg stood on the periphery, aware of his status as an outsider, but ready to be called in. Kane turned to him and held out his hand. "You don't need to be in this time, Greg. But I'd appreciate it if you kept your channels open for more intel."

"You sure you don't need any more personnel?

From what I've heard about this guy, he doesn't go anywhere without an army." Greg eyed the agents who were examining the equipment and lowered his voice. "I know they have experience, but those DEA folks don't like playing outside of their rule-book, buddy."

Kane hid a smile at the southern twang in Greg's voice as he reassured him. "We don't need a lot of heads for spotters."

"Gotcha. I'll let you know if I come up with any more info."

Kane walked with him toward his truck, a dust-covered monster with a hitch on the back and a cow catcher on the front. "I have a couple other names for you to be on the lookout for." He quickly filled Greg in on the other two drug leaders and then headed back to the hangar. Rivera, true to form, had sussed out the nervous agent and was buddying up to him. Franklin, on the other hand, had taken the female agent under his wing. Or was trying to. The woman, curvy, with a round face and a stubborn expression, was facing off with him over a scoped rifle. "I was a marksman in the Army, buster. I can shoot a pimple off your butt if you'll drop those trous."

Kane chuckled at his agent's expression and came to a halt next to Elise who was eyeing the pair with a grin. "He doesn't know Mackensie was a sniper in the Army," she said and turned her gaze to

Kane. "If she ever leaves the agency, you need to snatch her up for your team."

"I just might. Except it looks like Bear's in love," he nodded toward Franklin who was staring at Mackensie with fascination.

She shook her head then put her fingers to her mouth and let out an ear-piercing whistle. "Listen up. We're going to review the op and get moving. Enough socializing."

The team gathered around and eyed Kane and Elise. He let her take the lead, knowing she needed the assertion.

"Felix Varela is the South American connection in a triad of leaders that are involved in distributing drugs to overseas military bases. This operation is as big as some small countries' governments and has more monies involved than any of them. Varela was chosen as a target for arrest by the DEA because he's been the most visible, moving in and out of the country on a regular basis."

She shifted her stance, showing some tension. "Several middlemen, as well as smaller operators, have been apprehended as a result of DEA, FBI, and private agencies' cooperation, and we got the names we needed. We feel, we hope, that the kingpins are regrouping and may have some vulnerability, although you should know that multiple operations have tried and failed to connect."

Kane lifted his head and spoke then. "Shadow

Ops has been interested in this investigation for several months and has followed it closely. This isn't the first time we've been involved, either directly or peripherally. However, this time, I'm putting everything in, my manpower," he nodded toward Franklin and Rivera, "my resources, and even myself." He sent what only could be called a sinister grin around the room, letting everyone know his intentions. "And I don't intend to come out of this empty-handed."

A round of hooyah sounded from his men and, not surprisingly, Mackensie, who stood in a soldier's at ease stance. The other two men nodded seriously. Kane noted the nervous Nelly was clenching his fists over and over. To brace himself?

Elise added. "You should know this, especially my agents. What we're going to engage in over the next few hours will probably skirt or raze the rules we've been working with but it's imperative we get Varela. And on a more personal note, he's responsible for Garcia and Anderson being in the hospital." She sent a steady gaze to her agents. "I'm not coming back without this guy."

"Okay," Kane said, his pulse speeding up from the old adrenaline rush of an operation and Elise's resolve. "We're headed for the border. Varela was last seen between San Rafael and La Jarita but may be farther north or back across the border. I've been in contact with some friends over the border and they're going to give us some transport there."

"If any of you don't want to be involved, say so now. It's out of my jurisdiction and I haven't contacted our cohorts in Mexico, so we're going in without authorization." Elise waited for a moment then continued. "If you go, you won't be backing out without an injury. Whether it's from Varela's men or me."

More nods and Kane divvied up the responsibilities for coverage. He paired Rivera and Silverman, the nervous guy. Mackensie went to stand by Franklin who blushed and punched her in the shoulder. White joined Silverman with a grimace. "Guess I'm the odd man out."

"Can't interfere with the budding romance, bro," Rivera grinned at Franklin who gave him the finger. Mackensie studiously ignored the banter but Kane saw her grin.

They piled into two SUVs and headed south. Kane glanced at Elise, who was checking a side arm, her expression intent. "You sure you want to go through with this?"

She finished her task before looking at him. "I've worked for almost two decades to get these guys. This one bust will be the biggest and most wide-reaching takedown of them all."

As he drove into the night, Kane wondered at her motivation. Was it for more recognition in the

DEA? That was all well and good, but crossing international borders, being willing to assassinate a man, which he knew she would do if it came to that, even bringing her team into the mess with her? Was that all it was? And if so, why in the hell was he a part of it all, just to give her her fifteen minutes of fame?

CHAPTER 5

They drove miles from the city, past the wall and into an area that was protected with a high fence, topped with razor wire. Kane drove with the lights off into the desert, away from the fence, and came to a stop near a stand of scrubby trees. The other SUV headed to another bushy area and the team met in the middle of the road. Kane flicked on his penlight for a second to check the coordinates before quietly gesturing for them to find a place to hunker down and wait. Elise knelt beside Kane, aware of the river of sweat pouring down her back and into the waistband of her pants. The Texas heat had abated slightly with the nightfall but summer in the south Texas desert could still be unbearable, considering she wore two layers of clothing. She stilled her breathing at the rustle of sound and tried to see beyond their spot into the darkness around them. Nothing but shades of black and gray met her gaze until something moved. She poked Kane with her little finger, realizing then how close he'd been all along. When he stood she tensed, ready to fire, then realized he was moving easily toward the shadow.

She stood and followed him, coming to a halt at the sight before her. A short, stout figure greeted Kane with a melodious voice tinted with a heavy Spanish accent. "Hola, Kane. You were early."

"Anxious, Mela. This is Elise, my partner. Will there be a crossing tonight?"

Mela shook her head and Elise realized this woman was the Mexican connection Kane had mentioned. She looked closely at the woman, now illuminated by a half moon. Indeterminate age, black hair parted in the middle and pulled back from her face and a wide, toothy smile that took in the two of them. "Your man is on the move. He's still in Mexico but on the way to another gap in the crossing. North of here, about fifty miles."

"And how far away from the border is he?" Kane asked dryly.

Mela laughed, her voice loud in the dark. "About forty miles."

Kane nodded, reached in his pocket, and handed Mela something. She pocketed it and then touched his arm. "Be careful, Kane. This man is not someone to take lightly."

He nodded and cupped her cheek with his large hand. "Thank you, Mela. Give my best to Ramon and be careful yourself."

"I always am," she said with a grin and turned from them. A matter of seconds later and Elise couldn't make out her form at all.

"Who was that?" She said as they headed back to the SUV.

"A former coworker."

"Really?" Elise looked over her shoulder. "Military or agency?"

"Both," he said and continued walking.

THE TEAM MEMBERS reacted to the news that they'd have to travel more in a variety of ways. Franklin stretched and yawned, Rivera cursed and Mackensie blew a bubble of gum and sucked it back into her mouth. White and Silverman remained resolute and didn't react at all, other than to head back to their positions in the back seat of their SUV. As Kane and Elise loaded in their vehicle along with Rivera, Kane put in coordinates for the next leg of their journey. As he did, he heard Elise's phone vibrate.

"Fanning," she said and waited then uttered a curse. As she disconnected, he sent her a questioning look. "Update on Garcia. He's still in ICU, coded."

Behind them Rivera cursed again, his tone reflecting all of their frustrations.

Kane silently pressed his foot harder on the accelerator. He had to make it to the border before Varela did.

They were in place when the caravan of ATVs approached the border. Kane's heart rate dropped as he took a couple of deep breaths, falling back into the old ways of his training. He put his night vision glasses on, then honed in on the vehicles. Damn it.

Four, no five ATVs were making their way to the isolated stretch of border. Earlier recon had revealed a break in the steel fence so recently constructed and guardsmen were conspicuously absent from both nations. Lots of money had been spent on this gateway to the north.

And on each of the ATVs sat at least two children five years and younger from the looks of them. In the middle of the pack, a man dressed in jeans and a t-shirt sat, his eyes straight ahead. Kane didn't turn his head but spoke in an almost silent whisper. "Middle vehicle, in the back."

Elise stretched out beside him, her rifle trained on the man, responded. "That's the bastard."

Kane keyed into his communication three clicks. Stay. He lowered his head until his mouth brushed Elise's ear. "Kids."

"Yeah."

"Advance?"

"Not yet. Wait til he moves."

Kane knew she didn't want any collateral damage, and neither did he. But how did he manage the kids? He could take out Varela in daylight but he didn't trust his aim at night. As for Mackensie, he didn't know her record or her limits. Was she willing to do the job now? He asked Elise, unsurprised when she hissed, "No. It's not her job."

They waited for what seemed an eternity as the all-terrain vehicles with people hanging onto the sides, they were so full, made their slow path across the ruts and natural dips of the desert to the fence. At the edge of the fence, people started to climb from the vehicles when a sharp but low voice commanded them to stay in place. Varela wasn't taking any chances, either with Mexican enemies or US. Kane heard Elise's whispered curse as they watched Varela pick up a squalling toddler and hold him against his chest. He got down from the ATV and waited as two other men grabbed more kids and flanked him in front and back.

The odd trio, accompanied by cries and screams from the babies and silent mothers trailing behind, made their way to the break in the fence. As they did, Kane listened to Elise then gave another series of clicks, indicating slow forward. He and Elise moved in silence toward the break from the south, with the other team members moving from the north and west. As he crept closer, Kane caught the motion of one of the women as she broke away from the pack and ran to Varela's side. She grabbed at the little boy in his arms with one hand and lifted the other toward Varela.

The sound of a shot cut through the night and the other migrants dropped to the ground. The little boy fell onto the dirt as the forward guard whirled and struck out at the woman. She went down with a cry and the sharp tang of blood filtered through the night air.

"Bastard," Elise spat and made a couple of feet headway on her belly, anxious to get to the child, but more anxious to eliminate the threat of Varela. Her target broke into a shuffle at the sound of the gunshot, his hold on the kid apparently tightening, as it screamed louder. The front flank, realizing his boss was outrunning him, turned to survey the people on the ground. The rear guard lifted his pistol and aimed it at the young boy at his feet.

Another shot rang out, this time from the US side of the border. Elise knew it was Silverman. He'd never let the kid be hurt, but he'd just screwed their op. "Send them!" she said in a normal tone and Kane barked orders over his comm device. Elise stood and ran, her eyes only on Varela. She sensed Kane at her side, his firearm spouting shots as he covered her advance. Spurts of dirt and rock sprang up around her but she didn't pay attention to the fact that there were bullets behind those disturbances. Her attention was solely on the man who'd almost killed her friend.

White yelled something and another voice answered him, but Elise couldn't make out the words from the roaring in her ears. She made eye contact with Varela's cold gaze when someone tackled her and her face hit the dirt. Aware of the pain, but determined not to give in to it, she twisted her arm and brought her elbow up, connecting with a soft midsection. As she turned, the faint gleam of steel caught her eye and she lifted her arm in defense, hissing at the sharp burn of pain.

She avoided the next swipe at her face, bringing her knee up and catching the guard in the crotch. He groaned but didn't shift until he was bodily picked up and tossed aside. When he hit the ground, Elise heard a thunk and wasn't surprised when he didn't move to rise.

She glanced up to see Bear Franklin hold his hand out to her. "You okay?"

She nodded breathlessly, determined to ignore the pain in her arm, as well as the blood that was dripping from it. "Get Varela."

He nodded and turned away, only to curse loudly. "Boss!"

Elise saw Bear run toward the downed man as

the word registered. Kane was down? And where was Varela?

She whirled, looking for the squat figure but without success. As she twisted to get a better view, she realized she'd lost her night vision glasses. "Where's Varela?" she shouted at Mackensie as the woman ran past her, her sidearm in her hand, no rifle in sight.

"Took off in another ATV after his henchmen started shooting the migrants." Mackensie drew to a halt and raised her own glasses. "Ma'am? You okay?"

"I'm fine, damnit. I'm fine." Elise thrust her arm into a straight position at her side only to hiss in a breath. "I have a knife slash on my arm, but it's not critical. Casualties?"

"Mr. Kane's the only other injury. I'll see about the civilians." Mackensie headed toward the still kneeling and keening immigrants, disregarding the border fence she strode through.

Elise headed to Kane, aware that Rivera and Franklin were at his side and tending to him. White and Silverman were on the periphery of the scene, Silverman carrying two rifles, White standing guard. From both men's stances, Elise took heart that they were alert and capable.

She knelt beside Kane, her gaze on his face. He grimaced at something Bear did then looked up at her. "That guy get you?"

"Only a cut," she said and angled her body so he wouldn't be able to see her.

"Let me see," he reached out then pulled back, wincing.

"What happened to you?" She glanced at Rivera who nodded. "He got a glancing shot on his neck, right where the vest strap ends. It's bleeding but not too bad. Don't think it hit bone. A little to the north and we'd be singing a different tune."

Kane waved him away and sat up then held his hand out to Elise. "Let me see."

She wavered then held out her arm. A steady trickle of blood was dripping from her arm and the stinging pain had intensified with the drop in adrenaline. Rivera moved to her side, a medic kit opened. She let him minister to her as she filled Kane in on Varela.

"Well, hell." He said and glanced over to the still body of her attacker. "Him?"

"I uh, tossed him over there. Think he hit a rock when he landed. Side of his head's caved in." Franklin said, unapologetically.

"The hostages?"

"You think they were hostages?" Elise said as she watched Rivera expertly roll a bandage around her arm.

"He didn't let them move until he was clear, so yeah, I do. How many casualties from them?"

Mackensie had jogged over to them by then

and, keeping her eyes on the south, reported. "Three deaths. The little boy the guard was holding, the mother, or the woman with the gun. And a man, one of the drivers. Four others have gunshot wounds."

Kane sighed and looked at Elise. "I say we give them a choice. We call immigration and tell them they were being robbed or they head back the way they came."

"After we ask them a few questions. You know Spanish?"

He shook his head, "Only enough to order off the menu. You?"

"High school but it'll do."

"Hello," Rivera said, his tone dry. "You know my last name, right? What do you want to know?"

"And I'm pretty good, too," Mackensie said.

"Find out what they know about Varela and the situation they were in then give them the options Kane mentioned."

She sat against a rock, her arm cradled at her side and Kane beside her. White's search of the guard's body revealed nothing, as they all suspected. He and Silverman started policing the area, using their penlights to retrieve any ammo from their weapons, though Elise figured there wouldn't be much searching if the migrants held with their story of attempted robbery and murder.

By the time Mackensie and Rivera walked

toward them with their report, the ATVs were headed back south, full of migrants. "They don't want any of this," Mackensie waved her hand at the scene.

Elise's surprise must have shown on her face because Rivera nodded. "Said they'd be better off going back to their own homes in Mexico rather than face Varela up north. The woman who drew the gun was hired, or maybe coerced, by one of Varela's past associates. That wasn't her son the guard was holding, either. Nobody knows who the kid was." He ended his sentence with true grief in his tone.

"The whole group was walking in the desert when she joined them with the kid. One of the women knew her, knew she didn't have kids and asked where he'd come from. She didn't say and they got picked up by Varela and his men shortly after. Varela offered to pay them to travel with him. When they got going, though, they found out who he was and wanted to leave the ATVs and take their chances. He threatened them, shot a man they left in the desert, and headed here."

"And they decided to go back. Huh. I guess the sparkle is leaving the US for them." Kane said softly.

"And the fact that Varela is on this side of the border doesn't make it more appealing," Elise said then put her hand on his forearm. "He's in the US."

He tilted his head then winced. "If there's a bright spot to this whole crapshow I guess that's it."

They piled into the SUVs, leaving behind four bodies and what would certainly be a lot of questions, if the authorities ever found them, and headed back to Laredo.

CHAPTER 6

THE CLINIC where they were treated was a private one and Kane had to fend off Elise's questions about the legality of the whole situation. He winced as he watched her arm get stitched up, unaware of his own injury until they started cleaning it. "Damn, that hurts," he flinched away from the nurse.

"Hold still," she pulled at his arm to get him back in position. "You're lucky. You don't need stitches. But if I don't get this cleaned, it'll get infected and nobody will be happy."

Greg Jacobs stood in the opened doorway of the treatment room in his classic stance, arms crossed over his chest. As he watched them, Kane was sure he was accumulating questions to ask and figured Hank would know about the incident by now too. Greg was nothing if not effective in his communication.

Elise had requested another blouse, as hers was stained with blood and she glanced up in relief when Silverman brought in a bag. "Thanks, Aaron."

He nodded and shuffled slightly, "I'm sorry about earlier tonight, ma'am."

She gave him a sharp look. "We'll talk about it after I've changed, okay? Meet me outside."

She gave the nurse a small smile and asked for the restroom, then left to change.

Grateful he didn't have to muzzle the man in front of the nurse, Kane sat quietly until she was finished and accepted the vial of antibiotic ointment and bandages. "Here are some bandages for the lady. Make sure she keeps that arm dry and clean. No showers without covering the bandages."

"Will do, thanks." Kane stood and straightened his shirt so the bandage was less noticeable. His dark t-shirt probably had blood stains on it as well but in the dark, it wouldn't show.

Their team members had waited a block away in the SUVs and as Kane and Elise walked toward the cars, Silverman tried again to apologize. Elise heaved a sigh. "Let it go until we're in the car, Silverman. You can ride with me if you want. And I understand why you did what you did. You had to make that decision for yourself."

"But it won't look good for my future, will it?"

He said, his whole affect dejected. He walked beside her, his head down and his hands in his pockets.

"You may want to rethink being in the field, that's all. You're a good investigator, but you have to realize, the decision you made tonight? Those are made in every operation we conduct in the field."

"I'm better at the console," he muttered and then lifted his head, his eyes narrowing. "I'm good at the console."

"You are." She took another couple of steps and then added. "And you'll be even better after you get back to Seattle."

He glanced at her then nodded. "I'll see about a flight in the morning."

"Maybe not yet," Kane said and Elise and Aaron turned in question. "If you're good at computer research, you'll be our liaison with Hank and Greg. We need someone like that right now."

"No direct contact?" Aaron asked, hope in his voice.

"No direct contact. Although it's a shame. You're a good shot."

They left the city behind them and headed to the airport. Elise groped around for plans. She needed to head back to Brownsville, not to Georgia. When she told Kane he looked surprised. "I figured that's where we were headed."

"You're going to Brownsville too?"

"Yeah. I'm in, remember?" He went into the hangar to arrange for refueling, leaving her staring at him, wondering at this man. This ruthless, driven man. When had she fallen in love with him?

DAWN WAS BREAKING when they took off, this time with White, Mackensie, Rivera, and Franklin in the passenger seats. Their weapons were back in Greg's possession, but the other tactical gear was neatly stowed in the storage compartment. As he took off Kane remembered he'd intended to inform Hank of the debacle that was their latest attempt to capture Varela. He had Elise key in the number and then place the phone in the holder. When Hank came on the line, he asked first about agent Garcia and Kane saw Elise's estimation of his friend rise even more.

After confiding her concerns and getting an assurance he'd keep an eye on Garcia, Hank then asked about their outing. "It was a crapfest, buddy. A total crapfest." Kane said and heard murmurs of agreement from the rear.

"What happened?" Hank's tone was nonjudgemental but Kane knew he'd be reviewing the tactics as soon as he heard them, pulling out mistakes and offering alternatives.

"Varela had kids as hostages," Elise said baldly. "We couldn't do anything without putting them at risk."

"Damn," Hank said.

They explained about the attempted assassination of Varela, the ensuing battle between the guards intent on killing the hostages and them, trying to get to the drug lord and keep as many bystanders as possible alive. In the end, Hank said, they'd come out as well as could be expected.

"Except Varela is still in the wind," Elise said.

"Yeah, there's that. But he's on our turf. And I've got connections in nearly every state in the country. And what I don't have, I can get." Hanks said with confidence.

"And we have a new member to liaise with," Kane inserted and explained that Silverman was going to be their contact person for research. He noted from the corner of his eye that Elise cast a smile toward the wayward agent.

"Great. I've been in touch with Senator Mitchell. He has Gavin and Rachel on it. I think they're making some headway. I'll send you their contact info."

"Good. Any other news on the investigation?"

Hank was silent a minute before answering. "Yeah. We had a death at one of the foreign bases. A military police officer was killed while trying to apprehend one of the suppliers in Turkey."

Mutters from the rear drifted up to Kane and he bit back a curse. "Did they get the supplier?"

"Yeah. He's in detention under heavy guard."

"Good. Is he talking?"

"Not yet." Hank's tone indicated he was sure the man would eventually cooperate and give information on the supply chain, but the question was, was it anything new?

"Keep us updated, okay?"

"Will do. I'll send the contact info now."

Hank disconnected the phone and within a few seconds, a beep indicated that there was a message. "Thank goodness for internet services," Elise said as she pulled the phone from its holder. She accessed the message and handed it back to Silverman, who pulled a pen and paper from his pocket to jot the information down. When she looked at him in surprise he shrugged. "I don't trust phones. I only trust my system."

She shook her head and retrieved her phone then placed another call. "Caitlyn? How is he?"

Kane kept his attention divided between his duties as pilot and Elise's conversation. Caitlyn, Garcia's wife, apparently had some good news because Elise's face lit up with relief and some emotion Kane suspected was affection for her colleague. "Give him my best, okay? Have you heard anything about Anderson?"

She was silent then disconnected the call and turned to her agents in the rear. "Garcia is better. His heart is functioning within normal parameters, whatever that means and there hasn't been any internal bleeding in over twelve hours." The three DEA agents expressed their relief with high fives and then Elise's tone changed. "Anderson has had to have a total replacement of the knee joint. The shot took out most of it and they're not sure about his prognosis."

"What's that mean?" Mackensie asked, her tone almost belligerent.

"It means he'll probably live but have a limp the rest of his life," Silverman said, his face grave. "He loves being in the field. He'll hate being stuck at a desk."

"If he gets to stay on," White added, equally morose.

"We don't know that yet. And he's alive and will get to keep his leg. There was some doubt about that, you know." Elise said, obviously trying to keep things positive.

"So, what's the plan from here?" Franklin asked, his deep voice sleepy sounding.

"We get some rest then we regroup and make another plan," Kane said, his hands busy on the throttle. "Everybody make sure they're buckled up. We're getting ready to land."

The area around Brownsville had several small airstrips available and Kane headed to the one he'd been most familiar with over the years. Buddy Haynes, an older man who'd spent most of his retirement funds from the military on prop planes and the hangar, hung out there most days, waiting for incoming flights, often with a rifle laid across his knee. When they taxied toward the hangar, Kane saw the familiar left hitch in a figure's stride and knew his old friend would be there to meet them.

"Well hell, look who's here." Buddy's weathered face broke into a grin and Kane saw his missing lower front teeth that the older man had boasted he'd lost when fighting a Vietcong over a gun. Buddy stuck his hand out to shake Kane's and then turned his gaze on Elise, who was coming down the steps. "Who's this? And why'd you not tell me you were bringing a pretty lady? I'd have put in my partial."

Kane laughed and gestured toward Elise and Mackensie, who trailed after her. "I brought two ladies, but you better watch your step. They're both a better shot than you ever thought of being."

Buddy's eyes sparkled. "Even better. You all come on in and get a cold drink. It's hotter than Hades out here, even in the morning."

Kane led the way to the low-slung building. "Think you can store my plane for a bit, have it checked out and refueled?"

"Sure, sure. I'll get on it after we get a drink." Buddy led the group to a small room in the rear of the building. The "office" consisted of a beat-up desk with assorted stacks of paper littering its surface.

Kane noticed a few bills with pink inserts alongside before Buddy shoved them under a stack. He shuffled behind the desk and opened an ancient refrigerator that held assorted drinks, a carton of milk, and other foodstuffs. "What you all want? I got Coke, some juice, milk, and somebody even bought some fancy water." Buddy held up a bottle of spring water. "Don't know what the difference is, water's water."

"I'll take water, thanks," Elise said and accepted the bottle. When everyone had been served, Mackensie asked to use the facilities and Silverman requested access to an outlet, his computer case cradled against his chest. The other three men wandered out of the office, expressing a need to stretch their legs, though Kane suspected they were going to reconnoiter the area. He introduced Elise to the old man and noticed neither Elise nor Buddy commented on the others not getting introduced or even acknowledged after they left the room.

He sat in a cracked leather chair and Elise took another, leaving the upholstered tweed rolling chair for Buddy. When they'd drank a couple of sips, Kane asked Buddy if he'd seen any increased private traffic.

"Yeah. I noticed several small planes go overhead over the past several nights. None landed here, but I've made myself a reputation of not being hospitable to certain types."

"No offense, Mr. Haynes but you're one man. The drug traffickers usually aren't afraid of one man protecting an airstrip."

"No, but they do pay attention when my proximity alarms go off, all of which are interconnected with a security system. I wired it a few years ago when the strip was getting too much use late at night." Buddy nodded toward Kane. "Kane helped me out with it. If a plane lands on the strip and the sensors are on, alarms go off in my office," he gestured toward a small receiver sitting on top of the refrigerator. "And in the nearest police station, which may or may not be picked up by the officers but still deters the traffickers. I can even set up that the alarms can be picked up by the nearest air traffic control tower." He grinned. "Best security I could get."

"Did we set off the alarm?"

He shook his head. "Kane radioed in that he was landing, so I turned off the sensors."

Elise turned to Kane. "I didn't hear you radio."

"You were talking to the agents about Garcia."

"Oh." She took another sip of her water. "So, you've noticed an increase in air traffic. Is there another airstrip nearby? And have you noticed any planes flying over before we got here?"

Buddy laughed. "There's always an airstrip nearby. Dirt strips are simple to build and to cover up as soon as they've been spotted by the cops. But I haven't seen any planes go over lately."

Elise looked at Kane, "They could have gone over when he was at home. It was after three a.m. when we lost Varela."

"Live here," Buddy indicated another door leading out of the office. "Got a bed, bathroom with a shower, heat when I need it. Everything a man needs and my planes. I hear the planes at night, can't help but. And who the hell is this Varela?"

"A drug kingpin we need to get our hands on," Kane said.

Buddy took a long drink from his soda then burped. "'Scuze me. I'll get on it. Varela, Varela. Hadn't heard that name before."

"Be grateful you haven't and be careful. I know better than to tell you to stay out of it, but be very careful. This guy doesn't care what he has to do to stay free. He'll do it." Kane urged then stood. "I need to make some arrangements for transportation. Care if I use your phone?"

"Go ahead, but you can take my truck anywhere you need to go. I ain't planning on going anywhere today." Buddy took another swig of his drink.

Kane laughed. "That rust bucket? No thanks. I don't want Elise falling through the floorboards on the interstate."

"Ain't that bad," Buddy reassured Elise as Kane made his call. She smiled at the old man.

"You said your planes. How many do you have?" She asked and saw the delight in Buddy's face as he sprang up from his chair and took her arm. She hid a wince at the pull on her stitches but let him lead her from the office to the main hangar, where two small twin-engine planes sat.

Through the tour, Buddy talked of learning to fly after his tours in Vietnam and getting a job as a crop duster. He'd used monies he'd saved in the military and worked to buy his first plane, then the next, then after his retirement had bought the land for the strip and the hangar. "Nobody wanted this piece of property back then. It was scrub brush, nothing else. But me, I saw a home for my babies and me. And now, everybody wants to buy the place, urban sprawl." He finished with a harumph of disgust. "I plan on being here til I die."

"It's a nice place. Do you have much business?"

"A couple of landings a week. Enough to keep me in chili and beer." He responded lightly then turned to point out another feature of the older airplane and Elise wondered at the love a man could give to something inanimate. If it were possible, these two metal and fiberglass birds were Buddy Hayne's family.

Two more SUVs were delivered to Kane at the strip and Elise boarded the black vehicles with a sense of inevitability. As she buckled in, she said,

"My headquarters are on the west side of the city, near the airport."

"DEA office?" he asked as he turned from the dirt strip to a two-lane highway and headed toward Brownsville.

"No," she said shortly. "I wanted to be at another site, so I rented a small house."

Kane glanced at her, grateful he'd forced the others to ride in the second SUV, no matter how crowded they'd be. "Trust issues?"

"Mole problems. We've had so many holes show up in this whole thing that it was getting ridiculous. I figured if I rented the house and set up my own security and personnel, at least I'd have control of a few things in this mess."

She gave him the address and texted it to the other SUV then leaned back. He focused on the drive for several minutes then asked her. "What did you mean by you wouldn't be coming back without Varela?"

"My job is to catch him. That's what I intend to do." She said, her tone short.

"And if you fail?"

"I won't be going back to the DEA." Simple as that, and she hadn't realized until now that she meant it. If she failed in this mission, this task she'd been given, she'd resign from the agency. Hell, she might even resign anyway. She was tired of it all.

The rules, the bureaucracy, and the inevitable politicization of the drug problem.

"And when you do catch him?" His voice was quiet, pensive almost.

"I catch the next one." Then the next and the one after that, and after that. She sighed and turned her head to watch the traffic as the roads began to fill with morning commuters, talking on their phones, drinking their coffees, and ferrying kids to school. Had she ever wanted that life? Would she ever have anything approaching that kind of normalcy? She sighed again, wondering at her mood. She needed a long sleep, that was all. Just a normal sleep.

CHAPTER 7

THE HOUSE, a compact one-story, sat in a residential neighborhood off the main roads. A chain link fence bordered the small spotty green yard. Kane pulled the SUV around to the rear of the house where a tall privacy fence separated the property from others. He glanced around, taking in the open area around the house. "Not as secure as I'd like."

Elise opened her door and climbed out, moving stiffly. "It was as much as I could afford at the time. I've got internal and external lights, cameras, and sensors so it's ready for intruders. A rocket launched through the window? Not so much."

Her tone said more about her mood than her words and Kane silently followed her, stopping as she went inside. The second SUV had pulled in and parked in the yard beside his. As the others unloaded the cars, he surveyed the area, walking the perimeter, taking in the security measures she'd taken. She had covered the basics but there was more that could be done to ensure her safety. He walked around to the front of the house, noting the empty driveways along the street. Everyone was gone during the day, work and school. Not bad. If anything needed to be done, it could be done in the early morning hours, before mail deliveries, service calls and kids returning from school.

He went inside the house, appreciating the rumble of the air conditioning as it worked to cool the stale air. Window blinds, down and closed, kept the heat out of the house and masked the reality that this wasn't a home but a home base. Computers, cases with various equipment, and monitors lined the kitchen area and the living room boasted pillows tossed onto the sofa, along with what looked like portable sleeping cots, folded and tucked into a corner of the room. How many people had she intended to sleep here?

Elise entered the living area from a small hallway and stopped when she saw him. "Sorry about earlier. I'm tired, I think."

"We all are. Is there food here or do we need to send someone out for it? I think we need to eat and then take shifts for rest."

She gestured toward the kitchen and he followed her into the room, where a coffeemaker sat in a place of honor. "I have coffee and bottled water, sorry, Buddy. I don't eat here much so I didn't keep anything else on hand."

"Where do you eat? And sleep?"

"Oh, I slept here, just not ate. I'd get something at a restaurant or hit a drive-through usually." She stared at the coffee maker. "I'd love a cup of coffee right now, but I also want to sleep."

He opened the door and called for the others to come inside. "Let's decide on food then we'll go from there."

Rivera and White decided to go out for supplies and Rivera volunteered to make breakfast. While they were gone, Mackensie stowed the gear in one of the three bedrooms and Franklin started a shift schedule. By the time the men arrived loaded down with breakfast supplies, along with frozen pizzas, ground beef patties, and chips, a pot of coffee was ready.

Riviera prepared scrambled eggs, bacon, and toast, and soon everyone had eaten their fill, including Mackensie who announced she was a vegetarian and needed the toast and nothing else. Rivera grinned at her and produced fruit and muesli, after which Mackensie asked him to marry her.

With the meal over and dishes done by Silverman and Franklin, Elise examined the first shift. "I don't need to sleep right now. Mackensie, you go first."

"No, ma'am. Injured parties always rest first, meaning you and Kane. Rivera gets to get a nap too, then you all take the next watch."

Elise started to protest then winced as she pulled yet another muscle. She nodded and headed toward the bedroom she'd used before, near the front of the house. When Kane followed her into the room, she gave him a look of reproach. He held up his hand and showed her the bandage in it. "You either get me or Rivera and I think he's already snoring."

She turned and unbuttoned several inches of her shirt then started pulling her right arm out of the sleeve, giving out an involuntary cry as the stitches pulled. Kane turned her around and started unbuttoning the blouse. At her protest, he lightly slapped her left hand away. "Your injury isn't going to heal if you keep pulling the stitches. And I've seen a woman in a bra before, so don't worry that I'll become a whimpering beast."

She rolled her eyes at him and turned to pull her arm, now straight and relaxed, out of the sleeve. A couple of brown spots indicated seepage and she frowned at them, her face close to her arm as she bent it to examine the bandage.

Kane quickly unwrapped the wound, taking a second to gently pull part of it from her skin and murmuring an apology at her grimace. She watched him through her lashes as he used a bottle of water to wash the area then applied the antibiotic cream and a square of cotton bandage. When he started rolling the bandage over her arm, he looked up and saw her staring at him. Halting in his work he looked at her intently, his eyes darkening. "Remember I said I didn't turn into a whimpering beast?" he murmured and she nodded. He leaned close to her, his breath on her lips then pulled away with a whine. Elise snorted a laugh and tilted her head toward her arm, relieved and disappointed that the moment was over. "Just keep wrapping."

He finished up and then turned away from her. He'd made it to the doorway when her voice stopped him. "Your turn."

When he turned and looked at her she was holding her blouse, pushing her arm into a sleeve. "I'm good."

"No, you're not. You need your wound cleaned and rebandaged as well. I heard what the nurse said about infection. Now, where are your supplies?"

She retrieved them and made him sit on her bed. As she worked, Elise relished in the smell of him, sweat, musk, and gun oil. His warmth radiated to her and the feel of his skin as she pressed the edges of the bandage home was smooth and rough with a day's growth of beard at the same time. "You need to shave, but not here," she tapped the area above the bandage.

"I will after I've gotten some sleep." His voice was quiet and a little raspy. When he glanced up at her, his pupils dilated, Elise knew she only had to lean down to feel his lips against hers. Instead, she uttered a whimper. Kane's lips curved into a smile then he lifted his head and covered her mouth with his.

Elise leaned into the kiss, wondering why it had taken so long to get to this point. His mouth, firm and warm, welcomed her caress and returned it with more. As his arms came around her hips and pulled her to him, she covered his shoulders with her hands and gave into the urge to rest against his body. Desire, long ignored or even forgotten, coursed through her and suddenly she didn't care about the case, catching Varela, anything other than feeling more of the thrill Kane's touch elicited.

A cleared throat pulled her out of the dream and Elise backed away. Kane gave a final touch of his mouth on hers and then, with his hands still on her hips, leaned to the side. "Yeah?"

"Nothing. Just wanted to know… Nothing," Mackensie edged from the opened doorway and disappeared. Kane looked up at Elise as his thumbs glided over her waist. "Want to explain to them?"

"Explain what?" Her voice, husky and low, gave

away her mood and she shook her head. "Nothing to explain. It's none of their business."

He smiled a slow sexy grin then stood. "Let's go see what Mackensie wanted."

They walked into the living area to a variety of reactions. White and Silverman looked shocked, but then they'd never seen Elise as anything more than an agent, someone who never bent the rules. On this assignment, she'd twisted bureaucratic regulations into a pretzel. Rivera studiously ignored both of them, though he hummed some Latin tune under his breath that Elise suspected might be a love song. As for Franklin and Mackensie, both stared at Kane and her as if asking for something. Permission to do likewise? Maybe, as Franklin stood close enough to Mackensie that his arm brushed against hers.

"What did you need, Mac?" Elise asked, her tone normal and steady, thank goodness.

"There was a ping on Silverman's search. He wanted to let you know about it before you hit the sack." A faint blush showed on her cheeks and she quickly looked at Silverman who gestured toward his computer.

"It isn't on Varela, it's on the American. Brown was sited in Salt Lake City two days ago but nothing since. Don't know if he's still there but he left a couple of bodies behind, if he's gone."

"Middlemen?" Kane said as he approached the computer and read over Silverman's shoulder.

"The police haven't made a connection yet, but I think so. The two had rap sheets and are on the DEA watch list for the region. Either they were working for Brown and needed to be eliminated or they were trying to take some of his territory."

"From what we've learned, the trio had pretty much put all their efforts in the foreign base distribution, had cut out domestic distribution," Elise said. "I'm betting on Brown cleaning house."

Kane nodded. "Let's get that info to Hank and Mitchell. Hank has more resources than we do to check the location out." He glanced at Elise to confirm, then added, "I don't want to spread too thin. We need to focus on Varela."

Elise and Kane turned in, along with Rivera after that, and Elise wasn't surprised when the door to her bedroom opened and Kane entered, shirtless but with his pants on. He pulled back the light sheet covering her and slid in beside her. As he pulled her into his arms and kissed her soundly, she gave a moaning sigh and smoothed her hand over his chest, lightly dusted with hair. "We're supposed to rest," she murmured against his lips.

"We're going to, but I wanted to sleep with you," he growled, his hands covering her panty-clad rear. "Now, be good and turn on your side."

She smiled and flipped over, her back to him.

He laid against her, his body flush with hers and the evidence of his arousal firm against her. When he laid his arm over her waist, she ranged her own over his and settled in, already falling into a deep sleep.

THE EVENING BROUGHT another report from Silverman. Brown, the American drug kingpin, had left Salt Lake and headed east. Aaron reported that the two killed had, in fact, had connections with the organization, both being ex-military. Hank Patterson of the Brotherhood Protectors had hooked Silverman and his own tech whiz, Swede Swenson up and the pair were in constant communication. Elise had had to order Silverman to take a break and assured him the info would be there later.

"But if we get real-time intel—"

"I'll monitor it," Elise said and chuckled when Silverman paled. "I won't do anything to the program or your equipment. Just monitor, okay? You know I'm proficient enough to do that."

"Okay. But no playing around with the program." Silverman warned with the first menacing gleam Kane had ever seen.

When Franklin, Mac, and Silverman disappeared into the bedrooms, Kane sent Rivera out to patrol and check security. He eyed Elise. She'd showered and wore another DEA uniform of dark pants and a button-up blouse. This time, however, she'd left a couple of buttons loose, revealing a shadow of cleavage. He wanted to explore that area, breathe in her scent, and taste her skin. When she glanced at him and smiled, he returned the grin with one of his own. "Later," he promised them both then headed to the kitchen and some much-needed coffee.

Nightfall in the Texas summer came late and they worked on trying to find where Varela could have holed up. Buddy called in with a report that a plane had flown over the airstrip early that day, an aberration, since most small craft on daytime flights took a different flightpath, toward the more commercial strips. "Anybody flying over my land in the day are either sightseers or up to no good and this plane wasn't a looky-loo."

"How do you know?"

"Flying too low. Looking for a place to land, I figure. And under the radar, too."

Kane got as much info on the coordinates as possible then turned to Elise as she sat at the kitchen table in front of Silverman's computer. "Got anything?"

She turned to him, her excitement evident. "Hank has a bead on Brown. He's in Colorado and Hank has a team on him."

Kane phoned through to Hank and put the phone on speaker. "You on Brown?"

"Yeah," Hank's resolve rang through and he confirmed the info. "I've got Jake on it."

"Cogburn? Good. How many on the team?"

"Four, plenty to do what needs to be done," Hank said, his tone absent.

"You in the middle of it?" Kane knew from his old friend's tone he had another focus.

"Yeah, get back in a few."

Kane disconnected and turned to Elise with a grin. "You want to wake them up?"

She shook her head and stood. "I want to find Varela. We need to get some info on the terrain and site Buddy told us about."

They worked into the night, their focus split between Varela and the operation taking place in Colorado. As they worked, Kane became more aware of the easy way he could be with Elise. She didn't push an emotional agenda, didn't seem to want to "talk about it" but as she'd pass him or lean over to look at a map on the computer, her hand rested on his neck or she'd lean against him, already acting familiar and comfortable with his body. He knew two things. One, he'd move heaven and earth to help her capture Varela and avenge her friends. And two, she was his and he'd enjoy finding ways to prove it to her.

CHAPTER 8

MORNING BROUGHT the team all awake, eager to get on the road and find Varela and elated that the operation in Colorado had been successful. Hank's call near dawn confirmed that Brown, along with three other of his henchmen, were now in DEA custody.

"We're sure there won't be any legal loopholes?" Kane said when Hank confirmed the arrest.

"We're never sure of that," Elise said. "But, assuming there weren't any procedural snafus during the arrest, they should make it to trial, at least."

"We had three agents involved." When Elise asked for their names, Hank provided them. She had every intention of finding out if any of them had shadows on their records. If they did, she'd make sure their superiors took them off the case.

"Good night's work, Montana." Kane grinned and Hank laughed.

"It would have been a lot better if I'd been there but Sadie would have had my hide."

"You had a good team and I'd bet you didn't take your finger off the call button til the end."

"You'd be right. I'm heading for bed. Catch up with you later."

When they'd celebrated with coffee and another Rivera breakfast, this time breakfast burritos and fruit, Kane filled them in on Buddy's call. "Elise, Rivera, and I spent the night going over topo maps and finding the most likely place they'd have landed. We'll take a look at the spot, though Varela is probably gone again."

They spent the majority of the day picking through scrub, looking for evidence of a landing strip, and generally getting frustrated at finding nothing. Finally, Elise cursed aloud and threw down the rock she'd been holding. "This is just a waste of time."

"Maybe not. If we expand the search grid," Kane started only to be interrupted by Elise.

"This is useless!" She shouted then gave a frustrated yell that brought all team members around from their work. She stalked around in a circle, tallying items off with her fingers as she ranted. "There's no clear evidence Varela headed here. There's no evidence that the plane Buddy heard was anything more than a pleasure flight. There's no evidence of a landing strip, let alone a landing. This is wasting time!" She ended with another shout and Kane arched a brow at her.

"So, what's your suggestion?"

"I don't know!" she yelled and then sat down with a plop onto the desert floor. "I haven't a clue. We've been trailing this bastard for months and we're nowhere closer to him than we were then."

She sounded defeated and Kane realized her journey had been much longer and with more obstacles than he'd realized. He went to her side and lowered himself beside her. He pulled up his knees and laid his clasped hands across them, staring into the west, toward the city and its ports. "Okay. Let's look at this from the beginning. Varela originally came into Brownsville?"

"He's hit several cities but always in the south. Brownsville, Houston, he even came through the Baja Peninsula once but he's tended to use Texas ports or borders as entry points. Before this last time, he came through the port at Brownsville." She stared into the distance then turned her head to Kane. "The ports. He's been a lot more comfortable coming in via the water."

"And the ports typically are more porous than the land. If he needed to travel, he only has to rent a boat."

"More likely he owns one, or several." She stood

and whistled her ear-piercing tone to pull the team in. "We need to focus on the ports."

He nodded then stood alongside her and started toward the SUV. This time, they would be on his turf.

A REVIEW of Varela's records revealed only a couple of leads they could follow up on. Through circuitous routes, they found evidence of two pleasure crafts owned by corporations or people loosely associated with him. "Probably used to smuggle drugs, too," Silverman muttered as he clicked away on his computer.

"Maybe. Or they may be held in reserve for travel under the radar." Elise pulled the Brownsville map closer and sighed. "This place is riddled with places a boat could dock."

"How big are the yachts?" Silverman asked and Kane replied. "Big enough to sail across the Atlantic and small enough to dock in any water without obstructions." He huffed a sigh. "Do we have any history of where he came in before?"

Elise shook her head. "We weren't able to get a bead on him until he was ashore and at the private airport. There was some talk about a boat docking near Port Isabel, but nothing substantial."

Kane straightened from his position over the photos and ran a hand down his face. "Okay. Let's backtrack. What do we know about the organization? It's history. Who started it? Are the three leaders equally yoked? Do they have beefs? Fill me in."

Elise stood and headed for the kitchen. "I need caffeine for this." She poured a cup of coffee and then held the carafe out in question. When Kane nodded, she poured his then went back into the main room. Silverman, his face inches away from his computer screen, ignored them and Mackensie and Franklin were out patrolling. Rivera had opted to take a nap so he could take a watch in between.

Elise sat on the sofa and tucked one leg underneath her, then pulled the other knee up and rested her coffee cup on it. "We interviewed the middlemen and found out the rough structure of the organization. Apparently, Brown was the first to start distributing to the military bases, only in the states. He'd worked his way up from peddling drugs on the street and then went into the military and continued his side business there. After a dishonorable discharge, for what I don't remember, he started building his business. He made some contacts and found Novak a couple of years later."

"So, Novak had the European connections?" Kane asked and she nodded her head. "When did Varela come in?"

"When the supply lines got tight back a couple of administrations ago. Varela's old boss got killed and he left Mexico and headed south. When he established his own cartel, he started systematically eliminating his competition, hence the animosity across the border. He had a napalm approach to his competition, going so far as to burn out a few of them, literally."

"When did they all three hook up?"

"Thirteen years ago." She said bitterly. Thirteen years of messing with lives.

"Damn. That's a lot of product."

"And a lot of money," she agreed.

"Were they equal?"

"Appears so. Novak controlled the supply, Brown the base connections through his military contacts, and Novak the travel. There were a couple of dustups about that one percent of profit left over and Varela ended up taking that last percent, saying if he wasn't delivering the product, there'd be no cartel."

"So, in reality, he has more to lose. One percent of, how much profit are they making?"

"At least a billion, probably more. We can't get a clear figure on it."

"One percent of a billion is still ten million dollars. Not too shabby."

She took a sip of her coffee then leaned forward and set it on the floor in front of her. As he watched her move, Kane thought of that body moving with him, in unison, and had to shift both his body and mind to relax.

"Well, that's one option. Maybe there will be another power struggle. Varela certainly has enough arrogance to think he can take over."

"And if he ended up demanding that share, he'd be a nice target for the other two."

They stared at each other for a minute before Elise turned to Silverman and said, "Do you have anything on Novak?"

"Bohan, 'Hans', Novak was born in Serbia thirty-eight years ago. Lots of dissent during the communist era and when Serbia, Croatia, and the other bordering countries broke away from Yugoslavia, the tensions worsened. Genocide, war crimes, tribunals, you get the picture. Bohan was growing up through all this, with a father that has Albanian roots and a mother determined that her son wouldn't be killed. She sent him to relatives in Belgrade where he started running with gangs that peddled ecstasy. Pretty soon, he had a thriving business and started moving up the ladder, even catching the attention of the Russians. To escape getting under their thumb, he traveled. From Croatia to Romania, Montenegro, and so on. That's how he made his connections for the ease of getting drugs through Europe. He took the name Hans when he was around twenty-five and has stuck to it ever since."

"Anything to indicate he's not been happy with the arrangement between him and the other two?" Kane asked.

"A whisper." Silverman turned in the straight-backed chair and faced them. "When Brown was picked up one of his guys was heard saying something about being sure Novak had leaked his whereabouts. The agency has been questioning them since but nothing else has come out."

"Leaks again," Elise muttered then rubbed her bandaged arm. When Kane laid his hand on hers, she continued to rub it. "It's itch.,"

"Good," he said and took her hand away, laying it on his thigh instead. At Silverman's grin, she tucked it under her leg and continued. "Let's see if the agency can press that lackey. Find out more. And we need to find Novak."

Kane leaned his head back and sighed. "And I need a long nap."

"You both do. Rivera's going to be up in a couple of hours. If you take your time now, we'll be covered again for the night." Silverman said, his gaze returning to his monitor.

"Not sure we need the coverage," Elise muttered as she and Kane headed for the main bedroom. "Varela is on his way up the coast in his yacht, probably."

"No doubt." Kane pulled her down onto the bed

and arranged his body over hers, smiling down at her. "I want a private room."

"You have a semi-private room, right here."

"Without a team of monkeys watching our every move," he said. "It's like having kids."

"I'm not old enough to have them as kids," Elise said, half joking and half offended. "Besides, we don't have time."

"I'd make time." He kissed her hard then rolled onto his back, his arm beneath her head. "Okay, sleep."

She turned into him and laid her head on his chest. Slowly, inexorably, the regular beat of his heart lulled her to sleep.

An evening call from Hank confirmed that the henchmen had been extensively questioned by the DEA and FBI. When confronted about whether they thought Varela or Novak sought to take over the drug distribution ring, both men had clammed up, but one soon started talking, trying to make a deal. "He said all three of the leaders wanted sole control, but none were willing to risk total loss of the operation," Hank said.

"With Brown's arrest, though, it changes things." Kane closed his eyes as he thought of his contacts in Europe. "Let me make some calls. Find out where Novak is."

"You don't think he's in the US?" Hank said.

"Not sure. If he and Varela go at each other, who knows where the final showdown will be. Varela has been in and out of the US several times over the past few months, almost like he's planning something."

"Or strengthening his hold here," Elise stood, knocking her coffee cup over on the floor. A small amount of black liquid crept along a seam between floorboards as she ignored it and walked to her satchel.

As Silverman wiped the spill, she pushed some of his notepads out of the way on the table and plopped her satchel down. Retrieving her own tablet from the pack, she brought up a map with virtual pins in it. She motioned Kane and Silverman over to the table. Kane brought his phone and placed it on the table, the speaker on.

"Look at this. I'd forgotten I even had this," she said, excitement in her tone. "We've got this much info on Brown and his US organization, at least the one he had in place when he went into business with Novak and Varela. See? Minneapolis, Atlanta, San Diego. All of these cities had Brown associates. He had at least two dozen major cities that were close to or had military bases. When he expanded with Varela and Novak, of course, it tripled their resources."

"So, if Varela or Novak are thinking to take over Brown's part of the operation—" Kane said.

"They'll head toward his base sites. His home territory." Elise finished with a grin.

"Or not." Hank's comment served as a pin in a very tight balloon. The silence that resulted couldn't have lasted more than a second but, for Elise, it felt like an eternity.

"What's the other option?" She asked, trying to sound cordial, not as if he'd burst her bubble.

"What if they are taking out the smaller sites first? Eat up the small fish, gather energy, and then head toward the bigger ones?" He paused a minute then chuckled. "Sorry, my kid is playing a game on the phone where fish eat each other for energy."

"A modern PacMan," Kane said and shook his head, though Hank wouldn't see him. "Maybe Novak would do that, I don't know. I've not reviewed him as much as I've studied Varela. But Felix? He's going to go for the biggest win in the shortest amount of time."

"Even if it takes more manpower and costs more men?" Hank asked.

"Even if," Kane confirmed and Elise nodded in agreement.

"So, we need boots on the ground where?" Hank asked, obviously ready to lend manpower to the cause.

"Minneapolis was his base when Brown started. It's not the biggest operation, though. That'd be San Diego." Elise studied the tablet again. "I'd bet on

Minneapolis, San Diego, and Atlanta. It's at least three of the four regions he had power bases in. He had a small concern in Chicago but I think that was ancillary. And New York wasn't a big one either."

"Too much competition?"

"Maybe. He liked smaller big cities, not L.A., Houston, or New York." Elise confirmed.

"I have plenty of contacts in San Diego, old stomping grounds. I can pull a couple of men from my Chicago connections to fly to Atlanta," Hank said.

"No need. I can cover Atlanta and Minneapolis," Kane said. "With my contacts in Europe working on that end and ours here working, we might get somewhere."

Elise chewed on her lips in concentration and then added. "We need to check Omaha, too."

Kane looked at the map. Omaha didn't have a pin. "Why?"

"Brown lived there as a teen. Joined the Air Force after high school." She raised her gaze and met his. "I know. It's a long shot but I think we might find something there."

CHAPTER 9

SILVERMAN HAD to be ordered to take a break again and went to sleep. Confident they weren't in serious danger but still alert, Kane had changed to watches from two to three over the course of a day, ensuring that everyone would get at least eight hours off and a chance to remain alert when awake.

The foodstuff had been replenished by Franklin, who'd brought candy and soda, in addition to the usual cold cuts and chips, coffee, and breakfast supplies. When he pulled a carton of vegan yogurt from the bag and offered it to Mackensie, as if were a bouquet of roses, Kane knew his bear of an agent was toast. The small woman took it and with a blush punched Franklin in the chest, then headed for the refrigerator. Maybe she was smitten too, Kane thought with a grin.

A call to Caitlyn Garcia reassured Elise that he

was slowly recovering, or at least hadn't had a setback. His heart was healing, his lung as well, and he was conscious more often than unconscious. At the end of the call, however, Elise learned that Anderson hadn't been as lucky.

"They had to amputate his leg," Caitlyn said, her voice cracking as she relayed the news. Anderson, Garcia, and Elise had worked together in the Seattle office and then came to Brownsville as a team on the Varela case. More than that, Anderson often brought the girl of the month to cookouts at Garcia's and Elise had usually shown up late, but in time for nightcaps and chatting. Now, as Elise listened to Caitlyn tell of destroyed arteries, infection, and gangrene and, finally, amputation, she remembered the tall, russet-haired guy who loved to hike and ski. And loved being in the field. She ended the call and threw her phone on the sofa, not caring when it bounced off the cushions and onto the floor.

Supper was a frozen entrée baked and served with bread and coffee and Kane and Elise cleared the dishes, using their time in the kitchen to brush each other's bodies with their own in a teasing game both were sure would have to be brought to a climax soon. For Kane, living in a constant state of near arousal was wearing and it showed with Elise too when she volunteered to do patrol that evening. When he offered to go with her she refused his help. "I need some air," she said and, making sure her sidearm was tucked into her pants in the back, left through the back door. He knew the news of Anderson's surgery failure was taking its toll and also knew the need for action was growing in the woman he was becoming way too attracted to.

She hadn't been gone more than a couple of minutes when the dog started barking. Kane thrust open the door and jogged out, his pistol in his hand. Elise was nowhere in sight but the dog behind the privacy fence was going wild, barking, and growling. Bangs and vibrating fence panels indicated the animal was trying to get through the wooden structure.

Behind him, Franklin said, "I'll take the north side." He crouched down and ran to the edge of the house before darting around the corner. Kane headed south, along the other side. As he side-stepped, his back to the brick wall, he scanned the yard. There weren't any hiding places, other than one solo bush at the fence, on the far end of the yard. He scanned the darkening yard again and sprinted for the bush. As he ran, he heard the bullet whiz by and dove to the ground.

"Boss?" Franklin yelled. "Anything?"

"One shooter, east," Kane shot back as he belly-crawled toward the bush. In the dusk, the shadows cast by the four-foot-high plant made it hard to see detail, but it looked like a shoe or a foot covered in black was at its base. A shoe that looked a lot like those Elise wore. He crawled another foot, listening for the next shot. None came but something rumbled by him, Bear.

The dog's barking, Bear's rushing and Kane's heartbeat in his ears filled his senses but his focus was on that shoe. He was three feet away from the bush when Kane heard Bear let out a yell and heard something thud against the fence. Taking advantage of what he hoped was a distraction, Kane raised to all fours and scrambled to the bush.

Elise laid at the plant's base, between the bush and the fence, pale and still. He quelled his impulse to grab her and clasp her to him and put his hand to her neck where he saw with some surprise his fingers shaking. Her pulse, rapid but strong reassured him she wasn't badly injured and he made sure she was secure in her hiding place then poked his head out to survey the yard.

Bear was sitting on a figure dressed in black and was steadily pulling his arm up his back. "You gonna tell me who you are?"

The guy on the ground cursed him in Spanish and Bear said. "Don't speak Spanish so I don't know if that's your name or not. Gotta tell me in English." A drawl that was totally not Tom Franklin was in his voice and Kane knew from experience this was Bear's version of bad cop. Either the shooter would answer the question or suffer a broken arm.

A moan behind him brought Kane around and he checked Elise. She turned her head, not opening her eyes and cursed low. "What happened?"

"You tell me," he said and crouched beside her, starting to run his hands over her body to ensure she hadn't been hit.

"I got hit over the head with something."

"Huh. I'd have thought he'd shoot you," Kane said and helped her up. She groaned and immediately began to retch. He pulled back but kept his hand on her shoulder as she threw up her supper in the bush. With another moan and a whimper, she put her hand to the back of her head, just above her neck. "What?"

"The guy Bear is sitting on had a gun. Fired at me a couple of times. Figured you'd been shot."

"Lucky me," she groaned and gagged again as she tried to stand. He pulled her to him and picked her up then headed to the house. As he passed Bear he nodded to him. "Got him under control?"

"Yeah, boss. Tell Mac to bring me a hammer, will ya?" Bear grinned up at him as Kane passed. Mackensie slowed slightly on her way to Franklin, zip ties in her hands. "You okay, ma'am?"

"Just dandy," Elise moaned and leaned against Kane's chest, her eyes closed.

Elise had to suffer through another examination

and treatment at yet another private clinic. When the doctor advised her to stay overnight, she refused, insisting whatever needed to be done could be done at the house. When he finally acquiesced, she accepted the pain relievers and concentrated on walking steady and straight to the SUV. When Kane glared at her, she tried unsuccessfully to glare back, then fell on pleading for sympathy. "I hate hospitals and that place would be worse. I'd be the focus of attention, being the only patient there. I'll use cold presses, take these," she shook the medicine bottle, "and get some rest. I'll be fine."

"Right. And the interrogation?" Kane asked, directing the SUV toward the house.

"Oh, that's right. The perp is at the federal detention center downtown." She glanced around her. They were going in the wrong direction. "If you make a left turn here, you can get back on the right road."

"I am on the right road." He passed the turn and kept going. When Elise turned her head to glare at him another surge of nausea hit her and she fought to keep her stomach from spilling its contents. When she'd finally gotten her body under control, she leaned her head back and closed her eyes. "Maybe I'll question him tomorrow."

"Right," Kane said, his tone mild.

She did rest, as much as a person who was awakened every two hours could rest. While she did, Kane focused his attention on the house's security and made sure White and Mackensie were monitoring the interrogation of the intruder. When White arrived at the house after midnight, Kane glanced up in question.

"Name's Spinoza, Gabriel Spinoza. He's been associated with the Brownsville drug scene for about five years, came out of the military, and went to work at the docks. Probably one of the contacts for the distribution ring, but he's not naming names yet."

"Why'd he target this house?"

"He said he was afraid of the dog next door and climbed the fence to get away from it after he took a shortcut," White said, his disgust clear.

"And the gun? The black clothes in a Texas summer?"

"He had a carry permit and we didn't find a silencer on him. Black clothes?" White studied Kane's own black t-shirt and pants then shrugged.

"They're keeping him through the night, though, right?"

"Yeah. He still whacked Agent Fanning over the head, so he's going to be charged with assault of a federal officer." White yawned. "I'm going to get a cup of coffee. You want one?"

Kane shook his head and stood, aware of the stiffness in his joints from sitting in one position for so long. "I'm going to go check on Elise then grab some sleep too."

"She having to be woken every two hours?"

"Yeah and she hates it."

White chuckled. "I bet." He turned serious then. "She's going to be okay isn't she?"

"She is," Elise walked into the room, her hair disheveled and blouse twisted where it had come untucked from her pants. "And she's thirsty." She walked slowly toward the kitchen, her hand touching the wall every couple of steps.

"Still dizzy?" Kane asked as he and White trailed after her.

"I never said I was.... Yes, I'm still dizzy. If I don't feel better tomorrow I'll pick up some medicine at the drug store."

She opened the refrigerator and extracted a bottle of water, holding it to the back of her head and then transferring it to her forehead. As she leaned against the open appliance, Kane went to the sink and, extracting a dish towel, headed back to the fridge. There, he nudged her out of the way and opened the freezer. After he'd wrapped several ice cubes in the towel, he handed it to her. She accepted it with a sigh and held it to her forehead. "I need two."

He silently made another, this time putting the towel in a plastic grocery bag and tying it before putting his hand on her arm and turning her toward the living area. "Let's go."

"I want a drink," she mumbled, her eyes barely open as he maneuvered her to the hall.

"I have it."

She sat on the edge of the bed and accepted the opened bottle of water. When Kane handed her the pain pills she shook her head. "It'll make me sleepy."

"The doc said it'd be okay and you need the rest."

"I'm tired enough to sleep. If I can take something without the side effects, I'll do that. I don't want to feel droopy and drugged tomorrow."

He found some regular medication for headaches in a hanging toiletry bag and brought them to her which she swallowed with another drink. She settled back on the bed and sighed as he tucked the plastic-covered ice pack under her head. "That feels good." When he laid the other, slightly damp towel across her forehead, she breathed a thank you and closed her eyes. Within minutes, she was asleep, her breathing steady.

Kane set his phone alarm for two hours and settled in beside her, intent on resting as much as possible. But when he closed his eyes, he kept seeing the shoe-clad foot under the bush and remembered the stark terror he'd experienced before he found her alive. Was he willing to do it again? Fall in love with a woman who led the kind of life a DEA agent did? His wife had been a drug interdiction agent in the military and had died as a result of her job. To admit his affection for Elise, a woman who'd been fighting the drug war for years, was inviting another chance for loss.

He laid by her, listening to her breathe and the occasional grunt as she shifted and caused a twinge in either her injured arm or head, and focused on rest. And thought about saying goodbye to Elise Fanning.

Elise wasn't in a good mood the next morning. She'd had to have her arm dressing changed and the sutures were itching, her head still ached, and she was hungry and nauseated at the same time. She dressed slowly, thankful she wasn't dizzy, at least. When she arrived in the kitchen, the scent of eggs and bacon assailed her and her stomach turned.

"Breakfast, Agent Fanning?" Rivera held out a plate and she waved it away, trying to smile.

"No thanks. I think I need something light this morning."

"How about some plain toast and coffee?" At her nod, he placed two slices of bread in a toaster and handed her a steaming cup of black coffee. She sipped and turned to find the table full of agents, all staring at her. "I'm fine. Just a little upset stomach still. No dizziness, just a dull headache and an itchy arm." She took a seat and set her coffee down. "I'm done getting injured. It's someone else's turn."

Relieved chuckles sounded and after he set the toast down in front of her, Rivera pulled a stool over from against the wall, perched on it, and began eating his own breakfast.

"We'll head over to the DEA office after breakfast. See if we can question Spinoza." Kane said, then flicked on his phone. "I also got a text from Hank that he wants to have a talk later today. He has some intel for us. I figured a couple of hours downtown and then we'll hook up with Hank. Sound good?"

Elise nodded and took a bite of toast, feeling it ease her stomach almost immediately. As the others discussed finds, or lack thereof, from policing the backyard, she finished her meal and then sipped on her coffee. "Anybody check the yard behind us?"

Franklin nodded. "I asked if I could have a look but the lady that lives there said her husband was out of town and she wasn't about to let anybody on the property. Has six-foot chain link fencing all around the perimeter, except the back, and the owner of this house put up the eight-foot fence to keep the dog from trying to come over into this yard. Big dog, looks like a Rottie and Pit mix, bred for guarding."

"So, no go on the voluntary inspection of that

yard," Elise said and got several nods in return. "Do we need a search warrant?"

"Wouldn't hurt," Franklin said. "If we find a silencer, it'll back up the fact that Spinoza is lying when he said he was out for a walk."

"A walk?" Elise reached and touched her head, where a nice bump had formed.

They filled her in on the intruder's story and she glared. "Let me brush my teeth and I'm ready to go."

The DEA office was in the middle of town with a nice greenspace around it. The low-slung, one-story red brick building had offices and hearing rooms, as well as interrogation and detention rooms but still appeared bustling and low on space. The drug business was hopping in Texas and this office was obviously struggling to keep up.

Kane and Elise headed inside the building and he noted she walked with a steady gait, her head held high, with her agent face on. He was damn impressed with this woman and, he had to admit, she was hot when she was Agent Fanning. And when she was Elise, too. He turned his attention to the agent that greeted them inside the building.

Compact and not as tall as Elise, Agent Freddie Rodriguez looked tired and a little exasperated as he shook Elise's hand and then held his hand out to Kane. "Mr. Reynolds. I'll have to ask you to go through the metal detector." He motioned to the device and they approached it. Elise placed her badge and gun in the basket the security guard provided and then walked through the gateway. When Kane placed his gun in the basket, he pulled out a permit and laid it on top of the pistol, then added a knife alongside it. When he walked through the detector and reached to retrieve his belongings, Rodriguez interrupted. "If you would step this way, Mr. Reynolds. We'll have to pat you down."

"No, you won't," Elise said in a hard tone. When Rodriguez turned to stare at her, she stood her ground. "Mr. Reynolds is a private investigator I've hired to assist me in my investigation. His company has contacts that I don't have and, as an agent, it's my prerogative to have him assist me in an interrogation. He's been through the detection device and nothing came up. There is no reason you should search him."

"You seem pretty fired up about it, Agent Fanning."

"I have a headache and I'm pissed that the man who hit me is going to go free if we can't find out why he was on the premises last night. If you want to waste time today, Agent, I suggest you find us some coffee while I start questioning Mr. Spinoza." With that, she whirled and with one slight extra step, steadied herself and headed down the hall, calling for Kane to move it. As he followed her,

Kane gave into his urge to grin. If Rodriguez had been successful in searching him, he would have found several nonmetal weapons on his person, but looking at the woman ahead of him, he admitted she was the most attractive weapon he had right now.

They found Spinoza in the interrogation room, his tanned face mulish and set. He looked at Elise with derision. "You feeling okay, lady? You look pale."

She sat in the chair on the other side of the table and Kane took a chair and moved it back a few inches, giving her precedence. "I'm fine, Mr. Spinoza. How was your night? Did you rest well?"

"Too loud in there," he said. "I'm used to quiet, you know? Too many people snoring or moaning in their sleep."

"I'm sorry. Maybe we can find better accommodations for you tonight." She pulled a notepad from her jacket pocket and extracted a pen, which she started clicking. Kane hid a smile. She was using his nervous habit for a different purpose.

"You were in my backyard last night, Mr. Spinoza. Could you tell me why?"

"I told the guys last night, I went for a walk and took a cut-through. When a dog started chasing me, I climbed a fence and landed in your yard, I guess. Then this big guy jumped me and almost broke my arm."

"And that's all that happened?" Elise said as a knock came on the door and Kane rose to answer it.

"Yeah. That's all," he said, his tone sullen.

"What about hitting me on the head?" She asked.

"I landed on something, but I didn't see what it was. Maybe it was you," he shrugged his shoulders and crossed his arms. Elise jotted down a few words.

Kane placed a file in front of her and she lifted it so Spinoza couldn't see when she opened it. She kept her smile hidden and closed the file and placed it square on the table. "You landed on my head and gave me the injury, you say."

"Had to have. I wouldn't have hit you."

Elise leaned back in her chair and eyed the man across from her. He was in his mid-twenties, fit and with what would be a handsome face, if not for his expression. "If I'd jumped over an eight-foot fence and fallen on a person, I think I'd have noticed."

"Climbed, not jumped. And I was scared of the dog. He about eat me up," Spinoza said.

"Really? I hear he's a mean one, won't let anybody into the yard. Only people who can handle him are the man and woman who live there."

"Yeah, he's a brute. Big, lots of teeth."

"He attacked you?" She pressed and he shrugged, "No. I outran him."

"So, he in fact didn't 'about eat you up'".

"He would have if he'd gotten ahold of me. Look, lady. I'm tired, I'm hungry and I'm ready to get out of this dump. I told you what I told you. Now, let me out."

"Afraid that's not possible, Mr. Spinoza. You see," She opened the file and produced photos of several objects. "We've found a few things in my yard and my neighbor's. The dog, Tiny's her name, loved chewing on the silencer, but we still got some decent prints off of it." She laid down the lab photo of the silencer, teeth marks and all. Then she produced a rock with blood on it and a strip of black nylon rope. "We also found these in the area where I was lying last night. This rock?" She pointed to that picture. "Has blood that is the same blood type as mine. And this rope?" She pointed to the final picture, "Appears to have been dropped by someone after I was struck."

"I didn't have any rope," he said and stared at the pictures.

"No? Hmm." She picked up the rope picture and studied it. "This looks like a nice length, long enough to tie someone up. Maybe their hands?" She laid the photo down in front of Spinoza, now noting a fine film of sweat forming on his forehead. "Did you know we can get prints off of nylon? It's fascinating, seeing the technicians pull the prints off, like magic."

He cursed and swiped at the photos, scattering them on the table. "I ain't saying anything else. I want my lawyer."

"Fine. We'll arrange that right now if you'll provide his name. And I'll let you go back to the detention center." She stood and started to gather the remaining photos on the table.

"Look, I don't need to be there," his tone had changed and Elise heard real fear in it now.

"You were fine last night," she said, the folder held at her chest.

"There's people who don't like me in there," he said, looking away from her.

"Still, last night—"

"Was before you came, bitch! They'll think I told you something. I'll be dead before morning if you don't move me."

She sat back down and tore a sheet of paper off of her notepad. "Write your lawyer's name down. We'll contact him. And if you want to be moved to a different detention center, you need to have a frank discussion with your counsel."

She waited while he wrote the name down and then turned, headed out of the room, followed by Kane, and then leaned against the wall after he closed the door.

"Think he'll talk?" Kane asked as he leaned

against the wall beside her. She nodded and turned her head and grinned. “He’s more afraid of Varela’s men inside than of me. He’ll talk.” She straightened and started walking toward the main entry. “Let’s get something to eat. I’m starving.”

A few hours later Kane and Elise left the detention center with names and a scenario that made Kane feel ill. Spinoza had been hired by a Varela flunky to bring Elise to a warehouse on the docks alive. He’d not been informed whether Varela would be there or if she’d be moved to another location, only to deliver her. When Elise showed no surprise, Kane realized she’d been expecting a kill order or something similar. She’d been on Varela’s trail for months and must have felt like a mosquito to him, irritating to the point of madness.

They arrived at the house to another text from Hank, this time to call him asap. Kane put the phone on speaker and, after filling Hank in on the previous night’s activities, got an unexpected response.

“Sorry. I got some intel that something was being planned in the area, but it came too late. If my guys had been able to intercept that message sooner, you might not have been injured, Agent Fanning.”

Elise leaned forward so Hank could hear her clearly. “It’s okay. We may not have gotten info on where Varela is, but we did find out he’s getting frustrated. It's nice to know it isn't only me," she finished with a dry laugh. Kane leaned back and stretched his arm along Elise's chair, ranged beside his.

"You got any other information for us, Hank?"

"Yeah, I do. There's been a coup, Novak is dead."

CHAPTER 10

"WHEN AND WHERE?" Elise asked.

"Near Omaha, last night. Probably close to the time you were getting conked on the head. Big uproar in the area. Hit the national news."

Kane leaned back and yelled at Rivera, who showed up in the doorway. "Check out Omaha for a shootout last night."

Rivera turned and Elise heard murmurs in the living area then turned her attention back to Hank. "You know any specifics?"

"A few. Novak showed up in Omaha yesterday afternoon. A security camera caught him in a fast-food place ordering some burgers, of all things. We didn't get any photos of Varela, but some bodies found in a section of town that had some empty warehouses and demo sites were identified as

Varela's men. Novak, six of his men, and three of Varela's found. No sign of Varela."

"Damn," Kane said and was echoed by Elise. "What're the authorities saying?"

"Drug gang wars, urban blight, cost of poverty. You know the spiel. The thing is, these guys all had good shoes, nice clothes. They weren't kids who lived in the condemned buildings or young guys sporting a lot of new, stylish clothes. Novak ran in for European classic, and so did his men. And Varela had his men dress to blend, so no flashy clothes, just expensive."

"The locals won't be able to keep this under wraps if the press gets wind of it," Elise said, her mind busy with options.

"Nope. I talked with Senator Mitchell and he's going to see if he can get some info from the statements the cops are taking from witnesses."

"There were witnesses?" Kane asked, surprised.

"Yeah, a couple that had pulled into the lot down the street to score some pot. Said they heard the shots and pulled out to leave, then saw some men running across the street. One of the guys had a weird way of running like he had one leg longer than the other."

"Varela," Elise breathed.

"Yep," Hank confirmed. "Now we just have to figure out where he's going next."

"Or we make sure he's going to come here,"

Elise said. Her expression made Kane's blood run cold.

"No." He said for the fourth time in as many minutes. "You aren't setting yourself up as a sacrificial goat to lure Varela to Texas."

Elise paced, her energy level so high she was radiating with it. The other members of the team, probably fearful if they put in an opinion either Elise or Kane would blast them, waited as their leaders faced off.

She finally came to a stop in front of Kane and stood, her feet wide and her eyes steady and hard. "It's the only way to stop this before anyone else gets killed." When he opened his mouth to speak, she held up her hand. "Hear me out. Varela is on a tear right now. He's determined to take advantage of the upheaval to cement his position as head guy. We both know his ego is such that he'd never think he couldn't handle such a big operation. With Brown in custody, his organization is muddled. You can imagine the players jockeying for position. With that, in addition to the mess Varela caused in Novak's team, he's in the perfect position to take over. And we're in the perfect position to lure him here."

"With you as the prize," Kane spat out. "No."

"With me. Or, even better, Brown," she quietly stated.

He ran his hand down his face and leaned forward to stare at the floor, his hands folded together and braced on his knees. When he stood and started pacing himself, a signal to the rest of the team must have sounded, because they all started moving. Silverman turned to his computer monitor and started tapping away, Rivera went to the window and stared out between the closed blinds and Mackensie and Franklin began rustling through tactical supplies.

Kane disappeared into the kitchen and Elise followed him. When she found him at the coffee maker, refilling the basket with a generous amount of grounds, she came to his side and leaned against the counter, facing him. "I'm not going to sacrifice myself, Kane, but I have too much invested in this. Varela is massing his forces, making sure he has enough manpower to take complete control. If he has the time to do that, we'll never get him."

Kane didn't reply, only moved to the sink to fill the carafe and transfer it to the machine. She laid her hand on his forearm. "You know I'm right."

He took a deep breath then faced her. "I know. That's the kicker, Elise. I know everything you're saying is right and the plan could work. And that scares the hell out of me."

He took her shoulders and wrenched her to

him, covering her mouth with his own. This kiss wasn't one of affection or teasing desire. It was possession and terror and it both thrilled and saddened her. If they weren't successful in this scheme, she'd lose him, one way or another.

By the time the coffee had finished, they'd discussed the bones of the plan and headed into the other room to flesh it out. Elise laid out her idea of getting Brown transferred to Brownsville and a less secure facility, or one that appeared so. Varela would be sure to attack during the transfer. If Elise's team were put in charge of the event it would give the South American even more incentive to intercept the team, as he wanted Elise as well.

Kane picked up on the plan. "We need to have at least double the manpower we have right now. I'll contact Hank Patterson and ask if he can send some of his bodyguards to assist."

"Bodyguards?" Rivera asked, his tone almost derisive.

"These aren't mall cops or guys that are used to celebrities and paparazzi," Kane said, humor showing on his face for the first time. "These are ex-military, mostly ex-special forces. They know how to do what's necessary to keep their client safe." He looked around to ensure no one else had misconceptions then continued. "With two teams in place, we'll leave Colorado, fly to Texas and land on Buddy Hayne's strip then drive to the city. We figure Varela will be at the airstrip."

"What about an airstrike?" Mackensie asked and when White snuffled a laugh she turned hard eyes on him. "You think the middle east is the only place that crap happens? Think again, dipwad."

Elise waved a hand as if to tamp down the tension. "We need to consider all possibilities, including someone trying to highjack or take down the aircraft. That's one of the reasons we're pulling in more than one team. With backup," she motioned to Silverman who wasn't making eye contact but she was sure was alert and taking it all in, "we'll be more likely to see more factors and account for them."

Silverman was still tapping but chimed in. "Does Hank have any pilots on board?"

"Several," Kane said. Silverman looked up then, "Ex-military pilots?"

"Not sure. Why?"

"We need someone who can do some tricky maneuvers, just in case. And radar from every point. More than the regular airport stuff..." He trailed off and returned to his monitor. Kane, frowning, started to speak and then refrained at Elise's head shake. "He's planning."

They discussed a few more possibilities, including the plane being sabotaged, the strike occurring in Colorado, and a couple more. In the end, though, they agreed the small strip outside of Brownsville would be the prime target. "It's too close to the port, to Varela's ability to fly in and out."

Kane and Elise gave out assignments and tasks and the rest of the team turned to their jobs of acquiring weapons and ammunition and logistics. When she turned to him and suggested calling Hank he grimly nodded.

Hank agreed the plan was a sound one, if not risky. "You think Varela will go for it?"

"I know he will," Elise said. "My biggest obstacle is getting the Colorado DEA to agree to transfer Brown here."

"Wonder if Senator Mitchell can pull in some favors." Hank's question was rhetorical. The Senator, having garnered a boatload of positive press and increased popularity, had influence enough to accomplish the task. "I'll give him a call after this. What's the timeline for pulling the teams in?"

"Yesterday," Kane said. "We don't want Varela to leave the country and start consolidating in Europe."

"Right. There are several men in place in Colorado I know Jake will be able to use. We can be in place and ready within sixteen hours. You think Varela will stay in the country that long?"

"He will if rumors start spreading that Brown is going to be moved," Elise said. "We can 'leak' vague plans while we're finalizing our own. You know how porous federal agencies can be at times."

"Right. I'll have the Senator get in touch with you and get Jake in the mix."

Kane and Elise sat back and stared at each other. "It's starting," he said and she nodded. "Let's just hope Senator Mitchell is as influential as Hank thinks."

Three hours later, Elise got a call from her superior in Brownsville. "I don't know what the hell is going on, Fanning."

"Sir?" She cast an eye at Kane, who was watching closely.

"You're to go to Denver and pick up Derek Brown and transfer him to Brownsville."

"Yes, sir," she nodded to Kane.

"So? What's the deal? You've been off the radar for weeks and now you're the chosen one? Brown is a big fish. What's your part in all of this?"

"Sir, I'm as surprised as you are. My assignment is Varela, you know that. It's why I got transferred to Brownsville in the first place."

"You and your cronies," he spat. Elise had known he was suspicious of her transfer and probably jealous as well. Any agent that caught Varela would have a promotion in the bag. And, even if he enjoyed his desk job more than the risk of the field, Russell Moore craved power and position. She took care in her reply, knowing he'd horn in on the operation if he could. "Was there a reason given for me to pick up Brown?"

"No," Moore said, his tone sullen. "I asked and the higher-ups just said you and your team were to go to Colorado and pick up Brown by noon tomorrow. Get it done, Fanning, then I want to see you in the office when you get here."

"Yes, sir," she said and disconnected, blowing out her breath as she did.

"Problem?" Kane asked.

"No more than usual. I've been a bad agent, not checking in, and so on. My Brownsville supervisor wants in on the fun."

"He's no field agent," Silverman piped in, his tone alarmed.

"And he's not going to be in the operation. He just wants the reflected glory," she said and rubbed the still smarting place behind her ear, where she'd been struck. "I'll handle Moore later. Now, we need to get to work."

They ate supper by cleaning out the refrigerator and cabinets of all of the food they'd accumulated over the past days of occupation. Though the mishmash meal filled them, Elise saw that most of them ate less than usual, due to the anticipation of the mission. "We're going to cover the night in four shifts. Mac and Silverman, you take the first shift, and Aaron," she made him meet her eye. "No computer during your shift. You'll be ancillary tomorrow, but tonight, we need to make sure the area is secure and the equipment ready."

"Yes, ma'am," he answered, his face tinged with pink.

"White and Rivera, you'll have the next, with Franklin taking the third. Bear, if you think you need backup—"

"I'm good." He said, his spoon of goulash halfway to his mouth. He was the sole member of the team that appeared to enjoy his meal.

"Kane and I'll have last watch, and we'll leave for Denver by eight. Questions? Okay, everyone that isn't on watch, get as much rest as you can."

She watched as Mackensie and Franklin started the cleanup, with Rivera and White joining in to clear the rest of the house of evidence of occupation. By the time everyone turned in that night, all preparations would have been made to leave quickly. She made her way into her bedroom and did the same, stowing all of her clothes in a pack, then started cleaning her pistol. As she sat on the sofa, a towel and the cleaning kit spread out on the low table in front of her, she became aware of Kane's presence in the space between the kitchen and living space. She looked up in question and he smiled gently. "I'm going to take a walk outside. I'll be back in a few minutes." He turned and walked slowly toward the rear of the house, leaving her staring at him.

He'd come to mean so much to her, she thought as she automatically went through the motions. When had it happened? When had she fallen in love with this enigmatic, dangerous man? And could she leave him after the mission was completed? Or did she have to?

Talking about her feelings, her desire for them to be together was foolish at this stage. The tasks ahead of them required everyone's full concentration and she needed the most focus of all.

Kane's entry came with the scents of summer. Someone down the street was mowing grass in the late evening and Elise heard a bird call as he shut the front door. "Ready to turn in?" he asked, his voice quiet.

She nodded, aware of the change in his mood, arousal beginning to rise in her. His light brown eyes were dark, his gaze intent on her as she placed her pistol in the holster and looped it over her shoulder, then closed the cleaning kit. He strode over and picked up the kit then held out his hand. She slid hers in his and they headed to the bedroom. Once there, Kane laid the cleaning kit inside her open pack and then pulled the holster from her and dropped it on top of the bag. When he pulled her to him, he whispered, "I don't care who hears us." She moaned and turned her face up to him, ready for whatever the night brought them.

CHAPTER 11

KANE WAVED goodbye to Buddy and noted his friend's expression before he turned and jogged to the plane. The ex-Green Beret would do everything he could to help, but as a lifelong Texan and ex-soldier, Buddy Haynes knew how easy things went wrong, even those well-planned events. The fact that this operation was less than twenty-four hours old made everyone antsy. What contingencies hadn't they planned for? And with Varela in the mix, anything could and probably would happen.

He went through the preflight check and then turned his attention to getting them to Colorado. With a noon pickup, they should have plenty of time to land, get to the office and then rendezvous with Jake Cogburn's team.

The flight was silent, other than murmurs of questions, an odd tense laugh or rustling from behind him and Elise. She sat with her eyes front, her back relaxed into the seat, and, other than the odd touch to her arm, now sporting a large bandage, rather than the rolled version, she didn't move.

Kane remembered the night before. During their lovemaking, neither had spoken. And throughout, he'd maintained eye contact with her, through the almost unbearable caresses, the kisses, the peak. Afterward, she'd whispered her love for him and he'd answered in kind. As he tried to keep his focus on the flight, Kane wondered, where would they go from here? He lived in Georgia and had a business that put a target on his back daily. She lived in Seattle and would probably be running the office by the end of the year, assuming this takedown went as planned. Her ambition and his risk-taking didn't partner well.

Would she be willing to compromise? Was he? It was a question for another time, he thought as he prepared to land the plane on the private runway. And, he hoped they'd have that opportunity.

Derek Brown didn't want to go to Brownsville. "My lawyer said I didn't have to go," he said, his face petulant. Elise studied him. He didn't look like a cold-blooded killer, one who didn't care whose lives he ruined.

"Then he can have Colorado request your return. You're going today, Mr. Brown, whether you like it or not." She turned and left the man cursing under his breath. As she allowed the door to close behind her Elise turned to the Colorado DEA chief and murmured her thanks for his cooperation. "Cooperation, nothing. We got the word, we send him out. Can't say as I envy you the task, Agent Fanning." The older man, a bit paunchy from years of administrative work, added. "You need any more agents? I can loan you a couple if you do. Don't know what'll come up."

"I'm good. I have my team and a couple of private guards are going to help with the security at the strip." She didn't want to tell him she had almost a platoon at the ready, between Brownsville and Denver. Hank had come through with several men arriving in Texas as they were landing and Jake Cogburn's men were waiting outside, ranged in the parking area, across several vehicles. If Varela wanted to take them out in Denver, it was going to be on the highway, she thought.

Brown, handcuffed and flanked by officers from the Denver office, walked to the SUV parked at the front. As he started to climb inside the vehicle, a shot rang out and Elise, standing close behind him, shoved Brown in the car and dove on top of him. As he struggled to roll over, she wrapped her good arm around his neck and pulled it back. "Stay still, dammit. You want to be killed?"

He didn't say anything but continued to struggle. She was winded and beginning to worry he'd wriggle out of the car when a voice outside the vehicle called all clear.

Elise put her hand in the middle of Brown's back and levered herself up, not caring that he yelled about mishandling. "I saved your life, asshole."

When she stood outside the car, however, she wasn't sure. A man lay on the pavement about twenty feet away, a rifle beside him. One of the agents who'd accompanied Brown to the car was on his knees and checking the body. "Who's that?"

"One of Brown's associates, we think. Evidently, they decided to try to get him back." The other DEA agent smiled, "Score one for us."

"Yeah," she said and then lowered her head and barked at Brown. "Sit up. We're leaving."

The team piled into the vehicles as Kane gave commands and soon they were on the road. When he glanced at Elise in the passenger seat, he knew from her expression she was furious. "Okay?"

She jerked a nod and said in a near whisper, "That was stupid."

"We should have expected them to try."

"That's the point," she hissed, "I was totally surprised. Dammit!"

"It's the only thing you didn't predict. We're good." He glanced in the rearview mirror. Brown sat flanked by Franklin and Rivera, his expression blank. Would there be any other attempts to free him? If so, the team was alerted and would handle it but the sooner they got into the air, the better Kane would feel.

The airstrip looked as it had when he'd landed, only now there was another small jet at the end of the runway and, if he wasn't mistaken, Jake Cogburn stood at the lowered gangway. Kane pulled up to the plane and got out, pleased to see the man he'd briefly met before. "Jake. Thanks for helping out."

"Pleased to do it. The sooner we get these guys locked up and out of the business, the better." Jake jerked his head toward the small aircraft. "This one has a little more power than your bird and we found us a pilot that can play around with it."

Kane frowned at the addition of another unknown factor. Not that he didn't trust Jake, but the drug cartel's reach was broad. Jake saw his frown. "I know this guy. He's okay. Won't steer you wrong." He turned and yelled and a man no taller than Mackensie popped his head around the opened door. "What?"

"Come on down for a minute," Jake said. Tanned with features that would put this guy firmly in the average category, the pilot moved with efficiency. "Del Burns," he held out a roughened hand and shook Kane's.

"You have experience dodging birds?" Kane

noted the cocky stance he'd always seen in rocket jockeys.

"A little. Three tours before I came out to turn cropduster." Del drawled.

At Kane's dubious look Jake added. "He's a fire pilot. Flies scoopers and drops water on blazes. He's got plenty of experience dodging stuff."

Kane finally nodded and gestured to the vehicles ranged around them. "We're ready to go when you are."

"Right. Just tell me when to lift off. I'm good to go." Del turned and headed back up the steps and into the front of the jet. Kane took a breath and held out his hand to Jake. "Thanks again."

"Yeah. Wish I could tag along," Jake said in a flat tone that belied his disappointment. He managed life fine as an amputee but Kane knew he regretted not being able to handle some of the more questionable missions.

"No, you don't." Kane turned and motioned for the prisoner to be transferred. Elise alighted, then took control of Brown. To Kane's chagrin, she'd insisted on being the point person. Which meant her back had a big x on it right now and would until Brown and Varela were both behind bars.

The plane took off within the half hour and soon they were in the air and headed to Brownsville. It was four p.m. and they anticipated landing on Buddy's strip around six, well before sunset. Transfer of Brown to the office downtown would take less than an hour, assuming they got that far and, if they did, that meant the operation would be a failure.

Kane forced himself to sit and focus on the plan. He went over it again and again in his mind, thinking of contingencies, of factors they'd discussed, of anything that could have been an oversight. Other than the failed coup in Denver, he thought they'd covered every possible situation. He desperately hoped they had.

Del didn't have to do any fancy aerial work. Silverman, who'd stayed behind in Brownsville, had been in contact with the Colorado team and had insured a web of radar sites monitoring real-time. Soon, they were circling the runway and preparing to land.

Elise sensed the tension rising in the cabin and adjusted her headpiece. As she did so, she subtly clicked in the code for stand down, hoping it would be taken correctly. A couple of deep breaths from behind her and a rough chuckle reassured her that the team knew too much anticipation was as bad as too little.

Kane had stepped away and into the cockpit minutes before and he keyed in a ready command as they began their descent. His arrangement with Buddy was that the old man would stay out of the way but keep an eye out for activity. The ready signal indicated just that. Elise took a deep breath and tightened her seat belt.

Franklin and White descended first, followed by two of the Colorado men. As the team moved toward the front door, Brown glanced around him, as if just seeing the team members for the first time. "Why aren't we at Brownsville San Padre?" he asked, referring to the main commercial airport. "There's too many of you." He whirled and stared at Elise, his face white. "You set me up, bitch."

She shoved him, "Just keep moving." She had to prod him to the door. Kane, behind her, touched the middle of her back and murmured. "Stay alert."

She nodded, not taking offense, and gave Brown one more nudge. As he emerged from the plane onto the small stairway, a ping sounded as a bullet hit the side of the plane.

He drew back, heading for the interior but Elise shoved him forward. "Down!"

Brown stumbled down the steps and she hustled him to the nearest SUV, parked at the edge of the runway. As she did, she was aware of spurts of dirt and rock flaring up around her. Her mind clear, she brought Brown to a halt at the back door. Opening it, she shoved him inside. "Stay there," she demanded and closed the door.

The rest of the team made it out of the plane, as

had Del. He yelled invectives at the shooters and dove behind the stairwell before rolling to the rear of the plane and wedging himself there. Kane was at the head of the car, firing toward the shooters and speaking into his comm unit. He turned to Elise. "See if you can get Brown to the hangar."

She stared at him. "He's in the car, he's okay."

"And Varela is still under cover. If you want the bastard drawn out, go toward the hangar." Kane bit out, his expression furious.

"What about Buddy?"

"He left when he saw the activity." Kane made another shot then glared at her. "Go!"

She opened the door and pulled at Brown, who was cowering on the floorboard of the SUV. "Let's go."

"I'm not going anywhere," he yelled and slapped at her hands. She finally reached in and pulled a foot, causing him to flop back on the seat. Adrenaline, smooth leather seats, and his surprise worked in her favor and she had him out of the car and on his feet in seconds. "The hangar. It's safer."

"Hell, it is," he said, his face stark and colorless. "You're trying to get me killed."

"Not yet, I'm not. Now let's go," She pulled on him and after a second's hesitation, in which a trio of shots penetrated the car on the other side, he ran toward the low hangar.

The main entrance was closed and Elise headed

toward a smaller door along the front of the building. Hoping Buddy had left it unlocked, she turned the knob and thrust the door open. Pushing Brown inside, she followed him and slammed the door closed then urged him forward. "There's a small office in the back. We'll be safe there."

"We'd have been safe in the plane."

"Not if they'd hit the fuel tank," she said, hoping the drug kingpin believed Hollywood blockbusters and didn't know his facts about bullets and fuel tanks.

He didn't say anything but kept moving, half walking, half jogging toward the rear office. As he did, his voice changed and he began to offer her money. "You ever want to retire, agent? You could retire tomorrow, you know. If you help me out."

"Just move," she said, her pulse slowing and her other senses opening up, taking in the sounds of gunfire from outside, the echoing quiet in here. And the odd rustle. Rats?

"I could just walk out the back of the hangar. I'm sure there's a back entrance, right? I can even tie you up, make it look like I overpowered you."

"Dammit, move!" she said and shoved him the last few steps and into the rear office. As she did, he uttered. "You'll pay for this."

"Yes, Derek? And how is Agent Fanning going to pay?" Felix Varela's voice, soft and lilting with his accent, filled the room.

CHAPTER 12

Varela sat behind Buddy's decrepit desk, a silent hulk of a man standing behind, his tattooed face belying his prison past.

"I'd like to take more time with both of you, Ms. Fanning, but the situation outside prevents that, so —" Varela raised a pistol and shot Brown. The man went down, a single grunt sounding as he landed on his face on the floor. Elise saw the blood as it ran from under his body and knew the wound, if not immediately fatal, was the man's death sentence.

She raised her eyes to Varela and tilted her head. "Me next?"

"You, next," he shifted in his chair and waved his hand. The hulk advanced and Elise's fleeting thought of resisting him disappeared as he yanked the gun from her hand and hit her on the head with it. As she went down, she wished she'd told Kane she loved him one more time.

KANE NOTICED the easing of the gunfire as soon as Elise made it through the door and cursed. Something was up. The South American's henchmen were laying down cover fire, enough to keep them busy but nothing else. He clicked his comm on and barked, "Bear, can you move?"

"Anytime, boss," came the low drawl.

"Head to the rear of the hangar and go in the office that way. I'm on the front."

Kane sprinted, low to the ground, toward the building, his old pattern of zigzagging coming back immediately. As he ran, he thought of Varela and his team. Suppressing fire, no sign of the leader, and the two main targets separated from their own men. Damn. They'd been set up.

He crouched at the door and as silently as he could, inched it open so he could slide inside. As he did, he heard a shot and the sound of a body hitting the ground, quickly followed by another thud. He made his way along the wall, dodging fuel cans and tool chests, all potential bombs to alert Varela. As he neared the office, he could see two men standing and watched as the bulkier of the two step away and the smaller man limp forward. Varela glanced down and with a sneer, moved, twisting his body.

Kane saw him shift his weight onto one foot and figured he was kicking, who? Brown? Elise? Didn't matter.

He raised his pistol and waited. When Varela raised his head, Kane squeezed the trigger and watched as a small hole appeared in the man's forehead. Varela's expression, shock and surprise, were etched on his face as he crumpled to the ground.

Bear's entrance and tackle of the henchman happened simultaneously with Kane's rising and running to the office. He hit the door and ricocheted into the room to find the bodies of Varela and Brown covering the main part of the office. Under Varela lay Elise, unconscious.

Kane pushed Varela's body off of Elise and checked for a pulse. She groaned and opened her eyes, finding him staring down at her. "Is it over?"

"It's over."

"Good," she said and closed her eyes.

OF THE MEN covering the hangar, there were two deaths on Varela's team and only Elise injured on theirs. Seven men sat in the hangar, tied and covered by Kane's men, except for Rivera, who'd been called into the office. He checked Brown, shaking his head at Kane. "He's got a pulse, but it's thready as hell. Looks like he got it in the lower gut. May have hit an artery, from the looks of the pulsing." He stood and went to Elise who lay half on her side. As he crouched beside her and checked her pulse, he glanced at Varela. "You?"

"Yeah," Kane said and stooped down beside Rivera. "Well?"

"She's out but gonna be okay, unless the concussion is worse than I thought." At Kane's look of surprise, he pointed to the reddened and swelling area at Elise's temple. "It's a more fragile area, so she'll need X-rays and probably a CT scan. And you said Varela might have kicked her?"

"Or Brown," Kane said and watched Rivera prod Elise and the resulting groan. She rolled into a fetal position but didn't wake and the medic glanced at Kane. "He kicked her. Add another set of tests for that but I think she'll be okay."

"Thanks, Teo. Go check on the situation, will ya?" With a nod, Rivera left and joined the others in the main area of the hangar. Buddy's arrival a couple of minutes later coincided with the DEA, FBI, and local police. He cursed, ranted, and finally gained access to the building after Kane assured the officials he was the owner. He made sure they were alive then went to inspect his planes, threatening Kane if either of them had bullet holes in them.

Kane let White and Mackensie report the incident to the police and FBI. While the DEA probably had an inkling of the operation, thanks to

Moore, they'd receive a more detailed briefing once the preliminaries were out of the way.

Varela's men were soon loaded onto a van and transported into the city. The criminal investigation team arrived and dusted for evidence, took fingerprints, completed initial questioning, and took possession of Kane's weapon. He assured them he'd be available for further questioning and then strongarmed the paramedics into letting him ride to the hospital with Elise.

She woke later in the night with a groan and a cough followed by a curse. When she focused her vision on him, she smiled slightly. "I told you it wasn't my turn."

He looked at Rivera, confused, but it was Mackensie, who stood in the rear of the room, leaning against Franklin, who answered. "She means it wasn't her turn to get injured."

Kane nodded and lowered his head until he was inches from Elise. "I'll let you beat me up later."

"Promise?" she said, her voice fading.

"Promise," he whispered and watched her eyes close.

He spent the night in a chair beside her bed, dozing for a few minutes then watching as nurses came and went, waking Elise, taking her vitals and generally making sure neither of them rested that night. The next day, filled with tests for Elise and questioning for him, drug by until he was able to talk to her.

"I'm sorry," he said, smoothing her hair back from her forehead and adjusting the ice pack against her temple.

"For what?"

"For not thinking the op through. Letting you take Brown to the hangar was stupid."

"First of all," she winced and lowered her voice. "First of all, you didn't let me do anything. Your suggestion of the hangar was correct. Varela would have expected us to do something like that. If we messed up anywhere it was not having the rear of the building covered."

He nodded grimly. "Also on me. I planned the logistics."

"You weren't the point man on this, Kane. I was." She sighed and stared at the ceiling. "I just wish we'd gotten one of them out alive."

He shrugged, "If we had, they would have lawyered up and may have gotten off."

"Unlikely. Both had records a mile long. If we hadn't gotten them for the military drug distribution, we could have kept them in prison for decades for simple distribution and racketeering. But, with both of them dead, we don't have any chance for intel about the distribution matrix."

"You think the organization will stay in place?" he said, frowning.

"I know it will." She struggled to sit up and he pressed the controls on the bed to raise it.

"There's too much profit to be made and, sadly, too many people willing to sell the drugs to equally willing buyers. There will be a vacuum for a while, then more rings will fill the void. Smaller, probably, hopefully. And more apt to make mistakes the agency can take advantage of but, still, there will be more."

He eyed her. "You should be happy, Elise. You accomplished your goal. Varela is out of business, permanently. And so are Brown and Novak. The ring's been destroyed."

She turned her head and looked at him then a small smile curved her lips. "I guess my headache and sore stomach are making me depressed. And I hate hospitals."

"The doctor said you could go home tomorrow, assuming you don't have any other signs of concussion. You were lucky it was Varela who kicked you and not his guard. That guy might have done some damage."

She sighed. "Home."

"You want to fly to Seattle tomorrow?" he asked quietly, fearing her answer. She turned her head to glance out of the window at the blue summer Texas sky then closed her eyes. "Yes."

. . .

Elise stood with only a slight hunch in allowance of her sore stomach. She slid her satchel over her shoulder and looked at Mackensie, who was staring out the window. "Let's go."

Mac stepped forward and took the satchel and then opened the door to the hall. When Elise stepped outside a nurse called her to a halt. "You have to ride out," she said, pushing a wheelchair toward the two women.

"I'm fine. I need to walk." Elise headed for the elevator and outside.

"You need a wheelchair," the nurse said, only to sputter to a stop when Mackensie stepped in front of the wheelchair's path and got barked in the shins. "She said she's walking."

"Fine. You need to sign a waiver," the nurse called as Mac sprinted to the elevator and they entered the car. She rode the elevator down in silence, already wanting to be on a plane and away from Texas. From Kane. Was he on the way back to Georgia and his compound? He'd said that he'd given his statement and the authorities were finished with him.

The ride to the airport was interrupted when Elise asked Mac to stop and pick up some pain reliever. Again, her head was pounding and her stomach roiled. She hadn't thrown up this time around but if the flight to Seattle was bumpy, she'd have no assurances.

The team flew first class, Elise upgrading them, almost maxing out her credit card to do so. White and Silverman napped in their chairs and Mackensie, seated across from Elise, spent her time texting on her phone, glaring at the flight attendant when he asked her to refrain at one point. Elise turned and watched the younger woman for a minute. "Bear?"

Mac blushed and nodded. "He's, he's something else. I didn't think I could miss someone I hardly know."

"I'm glad," Elise said. "He's a good guy." She turned away as she saw Mac open her mouth to say something. She didn't want to talk about feelings right now, not Mac's and Bear's and certainly not her own. She had wounds to heal and one of them hadn't been seen by the doctors' tests.

Seattle was wet and humid, as usual, and Elise soon settled into her normal routine of meetings and debriefings of the Varela case. She got formally reprimanded for the border incident, as well as for using civilians on her team but she also got a commendation from her superior, with hints of a raise in pay or even a promotion.

At night, in her spartan apartment, she sat in front of one television program after another, not paying attention. Instead, she drank wine to relax, did light workouts to ease her bruised stomach, and missed Kane.

Her superior called her into his office two weeks after her injuries.

"How are you feeling, Fanning? Any more headaches?" The overweight, balding man said.

"No. I'm fine, fully recovered." Elise indicated her right arm, covered by her jacket. "Got my stitches out last week and I'm good to go."

"Good, good. Listen, the powers that be are looking to start a new task force to work on the increased gang activity along the border. Your name is in the top two for leadership. I personally think you'll be getting a call within the hour, offering you the job. Just wanted to give you a head's up and be the first to congratulate you."

Elise stared at him. She wasn't surprised, not really. Her phone and texts were still busy with requests from politicians and reporters alike, wanting to chat. But the border? "Does that mean I'll be in Texas?"

"Yes. You'll have your choice of offices, as long as it's near the border. You're familiar with Brownsville, so you might want that office, but it'll be your choice. You'll be building the team from the ground up and going from there. You might even be able to do that job til you retire, as big as the issue is down there."

She thanked him and accepted his congrats and soon was back in her tiny office, staring at the flank of filing cabinets on the opposite wall. Each drawer had paperwork in it, now redundant since most of the records were on the computer, but each page was evidence of her career with the DEA.

Why wasn't she elated? She'd worked for this her entire career, to be in charge and be able to effect change. Now, she could really start to fight the drug war in the south, up close and personal. It was what she'd always wanted, recognition and responsibility.

And she dreaded the thought of it all.

The call came within the hour and she listened to the Deputy Administrator as he talked, his voice encouraging and even boisterous as he described the possibilities that lay ahead. She said all the right things and made all the correct responses, all the while feeling nothing more than desperate panic. After the call was completed, she left the office and then the building, heading for the edge of town and somewhere she could breathe.

She stopped at her apartment and, on a whim, put a call into the office. "I'm going out of town for a few days. Right. Call it sick time, I don't care." She hung up on the administrative assistant who was telling her she needed to put in for leave a month in advance and then walked into her bedroom and started packing.

The plane landed in Chattanooga, Tennessee after midnight and after renting a car, Elise headed south. Her GPS, the only sound in the car, reminded Elise that she had country roads to drive in the dark and it had begun to rain.

He had to know she was there, she thought as she maneuvered the compact car over small hillocks and through dips, following the terrain of the land as she drove up the one lane road. His security system would be first rate and he could even be following her progress on a monitor now. Except he wouldn't know it was her, would he?

She took a breath, aware of the shaking in her stomach. Ripples of tremors ran through her torso and she tried to calm down. But, this meant too much.

A light flicked on as she pulled into the driveway and her headlights found him standing in front of the closed garage. He wore a light shirt, khakis, and soft loafers. His scruff made him look more approachable and she prayed he'd be so.

"Hi," he said and came to the car, taking her bag from her.

"Hi," she rasped, aware it was the first time she'd spoken since she'd boarded the plane in Seattle.

"Come on in." He held his arm out to guide her and Elise walked in front of him, her focus on putting one foot in front of the other.

They entered through the front door and Elise was immediately confronted by a black and tan mass of puppy, barking and wriggling around her feet.

"He's new." She said and bent to pet the dog. As it licked her hand and jumped, Kane stepped around her and placed her bag on the floor.

"She. I got her last week." He went into the great room and sat on the sofa, then picked up the dog when she started whimpering. Elise followed and sat at the other end of the couch.

"How did you know it was me?"

"Mac called."

Elise frowned, "She didn't know I was coming here, no one did."

"She found out you'd left the office and said there was some talk of a big promotion. Said she was worried about you."

"And you thought I'd turn up here?"

He lowered his eyes to the puppy who was chewing on his fingers. "I hoped you would."

Elise leaned back and closed her eyes. "They offered me a leadership position in Texas. A big deal."

"Congratulations."

"I don't want it," she said, surprising herself with the words. She hadn't realized until she'd uttered the sentence that she didn't want the job.

"No?" He put the puppy down and shifted to face her. "What do you want?"

"To work in a craft store. To learn to do crafts. To garden. To live a life that doesn't include killing people or planning offensive operations." She looked at him, tears beginning to form. “I want a life that includes you, Kane.”

“And my business?”

“If it comes with you, I’ll deal with it, as long as I can distance myself from it.”

“You can live without the adrenaline rush of the hunt?”

“I'll learn to rappel, rock climb, chase bulls, ” she said stubbornly and he laughed then reached for her.

“And if I told you I’m in the process of shutting down the business?”

She leaned away from him, staring. “What?”

“I realized I’m tired of the stealth, the ghosting. And most of all, I’m through with distancing myself from people. I’ve had to for too long and I don’t want to anymore.”

She glanced around the room, taking in the masculine, expensive furnishings, then looked at him. “What’ll you do?”

“Farm. The land is rich and I can lease it out. Sell off my equipment, that’ll bring a decent amount of money. And if I have to, I can find something to do with surveillance equipment. Just because I’m going to be out of the spy business doesn’t mean I can’t set up security systems for people.”

“Spy business?” she said, her brow arched.

“It’s better than saying hired thug business,

honey." He looked at her, his expression turning serious. "I've done some questionable things in the past, Elise. And I've condoned others' actions, with my business. I won't sugar coat it, even if I can't share particulars."

"And so have I, even though my actions were approved by the government," she said and smoothed her hand down his cheek. "Are you ashamed of any of your actions? Do you regret any of them?"

He shook his head and she smiled at him and leaned her forehead against his. "Then the Shadow Ops organization is over?"

"Yeah, as soon as all of my agents are pulled and in country, or wherever they want to end up."

She kissed him. "We're both going to be unemployed, you know."

He smiled and stood, then held his hand out to her. "All the more time to explore possibilities."

The End

ALSO BY KATE MCKEEVER

In the Brotherhood Protectors world

Saving Sidewinder

Sinner's Redemption

Saint's Fall

Shadow Ops books-

Sympathy for a Stranger

Shadow of Doubt

Shadow of Fear

ABOUT KATE MCKEEVER

Kate McKeever grew up in the southern highlands and lives there with her dog and cats. She loves to read, write, and garden, though she usually loses the war with weeds. She loves writing romantic suspense and making life as difficult as possible for her characters. Visit Kate at www.katemckeever.net or at Facebook, https://www.facebook.com/kate.mckeever

BROTHERHOOD PROTECTORS

ORIGINAL SERIES BY ELLE JAMES

Brotherhood Protectors Series

Montana SEAL (#1)

Bride Protector SEAL (#2)

Montana D-Force (#3)

Cowboy D-Force (#4)

Montana Ranger (#5)

Montana Dog Soldier (#6)

Montana SEAL Daddy (#7)

Montana Ranger's Wedding Vow (#8)

Montana SEAL Undercover Daddy (#9)

Cape Cod SEAL Rescue (#10)

Montana SEAL Friendly Fire (#11)

Montana SEAL's Mail-Order Bride (#12)

SEAL Justice (#13)

Ranger Creed (#14)

Delta Force Rescue (#15)

Dog Days of Christmas (#16)

Montana Rescue (#17)

Montana Ranger Returns (#18)

Hot SEAL Salty Dog (SEALs in Paradise)

Hot SEAL Hawaiian Nights (SEALs in Paradise)

Hot SEAL Bachelor Party (SEALs in Paradise)

ABOUT ELLE JAMES

ELLE JAMES also writing as MYLA JACKSON is a *New York Times* and *USA Today* Bestselling author of books including cowboys, intrigues and paranormal adventures that keep her readers on the edges of their seats. When she's not at her computer, she's traveling, snow skiing, boating, or riding her ATV, dreaming up new stories. Learn more about Elle James at www.ellejames.com

Website | Facebook | Twitter | GoodReads |
Newsletter | BookBub | Amazon

Or visit her alter ego Myla Jackson at
mylajackson.com
Website | Facebook | Twitter | Newsletter

Follow Me!
www.ellejames.com
ellejamesauthor@gmail.com

www.ingramcontent.com/pod-product-compliance
Lightning Source LLC
LaVergne TN
LVHW050549160826
845677LV00011B/2239

9798846693821